The Widow and the Tree

a novel
by Sonny Brewer

The Widow and the Tree

a novel
by Sonny Brewer

MACADAM CAGE

MacAdamCage
155 Sansome Street, Suite 550
San Francisco, CA 94104
www.MacAdamCage.com

Library of Congress Cataloging-in-Publication Data

Brewer, Sonny.
 The widow and the tree : a novel / by Sonny Brewer.
    p. cm.
 ISBN 978-1-59692-333-1
 1. Widows–Fiction. 2. Trees–Psychological aspects–Fiction.
 3. Alabama–Fiction. I. Title.

 PS3602.R48W53 2009
 813'.6–dc22

                                                    2009028730

Printed in the United States of America

10 9 8 7 6 5 4 3 2 1

Book design by Dorothy Carico Smith
Cover illustration by Barry Mosher

Dedicated to the memory of James E. Smokey Davis,
Alabama Treasure Forest Association founding board
member, who loved to see his name in books
almost as much as he loved trees.

IN THIS MYSTERIOUS COUNTRY OF BACKWATER BAYS AND slow-running rivers where bull alligators rumble the nerves of lesser creatures, the widow's tiny house looked like a child's toy abandoned on the dark landscape. A faint smell of woodsmoke hung in the cold December night, and it might have been stronger but for the stillness that let the ghostly scent escape from the brick flue and rise straight toward the full moon. Viewed from the quiet river, across a broad savannah of marsh grasses, the gray ribbon of smoke looked attached to the chimney top, as if put there for lifting the house off the world.

Another view, from high above the bank of trees: A quarter mile downriver the curving shell of the veteran's 1960s Airstream caught and reflected the moonlight. Beside the trailer, like a winking jewel on the ground, a campfire burned clean with only a pale thread ascending into the black sky. There up the river just a ways, the bait house windows were shuttered until dawn brought boats alongside its dock and pickups into the parking lot and the sagging floor creaked underneath the shoes of fishermen and coffee drinkers.

Soon enough a stir of wind would fray the smoke from the widow's chimney, twist it into tendrils, make a man want to turn up his collar and tighten his shoulders. But now, these two men who crept along the path took no notice of the air's chill, only looked ahead toward a hummock fronting a dark treeline.

"You see Ghosthead Oak now?" the game warden asked, stopping to catch a better breath, pointing ahead. "Look. It's the size of a goddamn hill." The path had widened and the two men stood side by side.

"I see how you dragged me away from a tolerable Christmas party and some good Scotch whisky to go pyrootin' through the swamp," the deputy answered, drawing up short of a fence. "And I see a sign nailed to a post that says NO TRESPASSING," he added.

"To hell with the sign. I'm an officer of the law. And since your uncle bribed me to give you a job, so are you." The game warden lifted his finger, shaking it. "Besides all that, the damn tree yonder ought to be mine anyway."

The deputy looked over at the game warden. "By what design should somebody else's tree belong to you?"

The game warden ignored the question and led the way for another twenty yards. He wheezed and pointed. "Hell, are you looking, or what? That tree right there is Ghosthead Oak. Pay attention. You gonna be my deputy, you gotta know about things like a five-hundred-year-old oak tree in our jurisdiction."

The deputy for the first time took a gander over the scrub brush ahead of him. He saw the tree. He stopped on the path. He saw there rising from the moonlit sway of tall grass, a tree unlike any other he'd ever seen. Nor would he see its match along the whole of the Gulf coastal crescent from New Orleans to Apalachicola. For though it was a live oak, and such were plentiful, squatting the land, low and broad with their gnarly twisted trunks and furrowed bark like the hide of some ancient thunderous beast, there was not another tree the equal of this one.

Live oaks grew easily and spread their canopies wider than houses, many with trunks the size of whole rooms, and Ghosthead Oak was the king of them all in this backwoods landscape, or even those owning land and guarding bronze placques in city parks. The rough-barked limbs of the live oak before the deputy drooped under their own weight and length, dipping close to the ground at two-thirds their hundred-foot reach, the ends of the branches turning up toward the sky like the palms of a conjuring sorcerer.

"I wish it weren't the middle of the night," the deputy said.

"Hey, boy! Don't you be complaining about the hour. You're uncle might've leaned on me to give you a job, but when I say jump, you ask how high. When I say go, don't look at your damn watch."

The game warden leaned close, his breath whiskey-hard. "You got some catching up to do. Being a deputy is not like sitting behind that desk down there in Florida typing up stories."

"Oh, you misunderstand, boss," the deputy allowed, with a touch of condescension that got by the game warden. "I'm not complaining about our night mission. I just want to see this tree better. In the light of day." He stepped back when the game warden stumbled and pitched toward him.

"Can't say I think that's a good idea. The widow's a mighty touchy woman. Game warden's work can get dangerous when you least expect it. Hell, the sissy-britches county sheriff could learn a thing or two on my beat," the game warden said, patting the walnut handle of a pistol beneath his worn Harris Tweed coat.

"You ever get to write about some murder down there in the Everglades?" The game warden took a shiny flask from his coat pocket. He did not sip the whiskey, but took a swallow. Before twisting the cap back on, he offered a drink to the deputy.

"No, thank you. Bourbon's not my cup of tea." A breeze ruffled the leaves and the deputy zipped his windbreaker. "Neither was covering hard crime for the paper." The deputy allowed he wrote easy stories for the Tribune. "I stuck to features a mile away from backwoods poachers," he said. The game warden answered, "I got a subject for you here. Don't it make your typing fingers twitch? This tree's a damn natural wonder."

"I have to admit," the deputy said, "when you pointed

the nose of your Dodge Ram into the night

overtake the north wind down highway 98,

the call to duty. No, sir." The deputy shook his head. ᴅᴜ.

look at this tree. Jesus!"

"Yeah, I could tell you were skeptical. Me calling us away from the party like that. Time Fairhope fell ten, twelve, fifteen miles behind us you were tightening up on me. I could tell. When we left the main highway, I figured you might be composing your resignation." The game warden poked the deputy in the chest. "Which, mind you, I don't give a shit if you do."

"Not a chance, sir. Not when you show me something like this." The deputy looked up and lifted his hands as they walked underneath the canopy of the tree. The moon's light found the leafy ground here and there like flashlight beams playing down from somewhere in the treetop.

"You ought to freelance something on Ghosthead Oak. Been nothin' but crappy pictures run in the Gazette," the game warden said. "I might let you moonlight on the computer if you deputy for me like your heart's in it."

"Thanks, but my reporter days are done."

"You never know. Just don't let your fingers get stove up. I might need a writer boy one of these days."

The deputy lost the thread of the game warden's chatter. His eyes swept the breadth of the looming dark beneath the tree, as if sensing something there beyond the oak's visual dimensions.

"When I got a minute, I want you to tell me why you quit the paper. Or did you get run off?" The game warden chuckled, smirking at the insinuation.

The deputy missed it, and as midnight closed on the pair, he stood still as a mannequin posed in a store window, his gaze intent on the big tree. The deputy had become mindless of the game warden and Dewar's on the rocks and the girl in the red dress with a Santa hat. He was lost in wonder with Ghosthead Oak until the game warden said, "Shhh!"

Going to a rough whisper: "You hear that? Somebody's coming."

O N NIGHTS WHEN THE WIND WAS RIGHT, THE WIDOW heard most everything they said. The giant oak grew close by her cottage.

The wind-up clock on her mantel clinked and hummed, a small sound of springs and gears signaling it was about to strike midnight. She pushed herself up from the easy chair and, clutching her lap blanket to her chest, went over to the light switch beside the front door.

With a downward flick the room fell dark.

From the fireplace behind her smoldered uncertain light from scraps of flame and red embers. The wind blew into the room when she cracked open the door. She peered out and her eyes watered. She held her breath, listening. Usually, they carried no lights when they came. These crept in darkness and kept their voices low. Still, she heard a girl say, "My dress is caught. Charlie! Can you help me here?"

The widow pictured the trespassers, knew that barbed wire had snagged the hem of the girl's dress as she tried to cross the fence onto her land, and she knew that the young men of today were not the gentlemen of her past. Who knew where, ahead or behind, her Charles could be found?

The stranded girl would be on the path near the fence post where the NO TRESPASSING sign was hung, the usual spot where people got snagged going out to the tree and where their bravery and resolve were put to the test, fearful their trek to Ghosthead Oak might get them caught and shot.

The widow had not shot anyone stealing onto her property. Maybe she got a picture in her head of such a fate for them, those who came to the tree to drink their liquor or who thought the cavernous space beneath its branches was just another honky-tonk. But she never took down the .410 from its pegs above the mantel.

Her father, however, had peppered two young men with birdshot from the barrel of the same little shotgun and had laughed with Doc Baldwin down in Magnolia Springs when the doctor told how both fellows had whimpered like schoolgirls as he plucked pellets from their backsides. That event gave birth to the myth of on-sight shootings at Ghosthead Oak.

She could understand why so many were drawn to the tree her great-great-grandfather had written of often in his journal. In the lofty language of essayers from his era, he had suggested the sapling brushed the thick black leather of De Soto's boots. Her grandfather had also written that the encounter with the Spaniard endowed the little tree with a promise of greatness, that the oak was destined to live into that promise.

On a page near the beginning of the second volume of his journal, her grandfather had written: *Story keepers of the leather-face tribes, the people of the land before white men came, told of a coppery cold night during the tenth moon when ten thousand fireflies folded their clicking casements and settled onto every branch of the slender young tree, from its low knotty arms to its high and skinny pointers.*

But not one insect sparked its light.

Then, on some secret signal all the bugs caught their fires at once and they went on-and-off, on-and-off, on-and-off in perfect cadence. And from that time, when it had a living light in its limbs, the tree was called the Ghosthead Oak. With their strange rhythm of illumination, a burl had that night commenced growing on the tree and it would be according to its likeness to a dead man's head that its name would be remembered as Ghosthead Oak by the white men.

The widow had read the pages many times, and the story was like the words of a song for her. But one of her grandfather's journal entries bore a cryptic prophecy, a sentence she could see on the yellow, wavy page, beneath a date, July 9, 1871: *Blood, then, deep as the silver water feeding the taproot, will in those days bring down the great tree, render its twisted wood back to salty dark soil.*

What her grandfather meant when he had written *in those days*—if he had truly foreseen some future circumstance—was caught perhaps in a narrow cleft of his brain. Whatever it meant, such meaning had not channeled into his feathered quill. The widow could not make any sense of his prediction.

The ancient ones, her grandfather wrote, had been able to make sense of the very twist of a tree's limbs, could look at stands of oak and juniper, of magnolia and pine, and decipher from their trunks and branches the tale of seasons of sun and rain, years of windsong and tribal passings. But so few of the trespassers, the widow knew, really apprehended Ghosthead Oak's story, that the tree itself was a mysterious journal.

Any more than the family who stopped their Chevrolet station wagon for a photo with the Grand Canyon behind them before making a break for the hotel swimming pool had any real sense of awe for the miracle of nature over their shoulders. Most of those who sneaked across her fence did not even connect the name of the tree to the huge burl twice head-high on the trunk's south side, the bulging knot so like a forlorn face with wide-open eyes and down turned mouth.

That was because the trespassers did not see the tree when they looked at it.

Her father, on the other hand, when his eyes were no good and death was near, had asked her to take him not to church but to the tree and immediately upon crossing into its shade he had stopped, gripped her hand to steady himself, knelt, and when his knees bore down into the loamy soil, he bowed his head and muttered a prayer. Her father had not so much as said a blessing at a meal in her presence, had never once sat beside her in a pew.

After she had walked him back to the house, she asked him why he had knelt at the tree. "Why, all these years I have followed the beliefs of our Celtic forebears. I am a Druid, of course!" When her father stopped laughing and got back his breath, he took both her hands and said quietly, "I am simply abandoning my ego before an outward and visible sign of God. That tree is for me a sacrament."

That was why she buried him in its shade and was provoked, in due course, to learn something of the Druids, how they revered oaks and hazels among the trees, the land and sea and sky, stories of their human sacrifice.

She also learned, in due course, that her father had been a Catholic, found his card bearing such evidence, and wondered at his reconciliation with her mother's Baptist faith. He had kept his religion to himself, his only visible ritual the tending of chores and duties about the homeplace.

Now, it was her charge to see after the hundred acres left to her, to be the uneasy caretaker of the land, to pay the taxes and also grow some few vegetables for her table, to harvest honey from bees in the many vine-covered hives tilting about the place, and to remove the spoils of the trespassers who came more and more. The slam of their car doors was almost a nightly occurrence.

Tonight in her cotton gown as white as the cool skin of

her breast, her ankles cut by the wind knifing in through the door only just open, she could hear the young woman's voice as if she stood next to her. It sailed through the air like some nightbird's protest.

"Charles!"

Now her young man:

"I told you, Ellie, just bunch up your dress. You're gonna hike it up soon enough."

"Would you just quit with your trash-mouth? It's not romantic, you know."

"Sorry, El. But you have to be quiet. That old woman has shot people."

"No she hasn't."

"Jimmy said so."

"And you listen to anything Jimmy Fortner has to say? Come on."

"Hey," he said, his voice low and urgent, "hush a minute! I hear someone coming."

"What do we do?" she asked.

"Quick," he said, "hide!"

ᴇᴛ'ꜱ ʜᴀᴠᴇ ꜱᴏᴍᴇ ꜰᴜɴ," ᴛʜᴇ ɢᴀᴍᴇ ᴡᴀʀᴅᴇɴ ᴡʜɪꜱᴘᴇʀᴇᴅ to the deputy.

"Fun? We left that back at the party," the deputy said. "Did you see the girl I was talking to?"

"You only think you're missing out on the fun," the game warden said. "Just you hide and watch."

The game warden drew his service revolver.

"Are you crazy? Maybe the somebody coming to the tree has got one of those, too."

"Maybe. Let's find out." The game warden pointed the pistol toward the stars and fired, the explosion ricocheting through the night, collecting a scream from some female voice in the distance. The male voice was more of an agonized cry as if some pain had struck him.

When the game warden fired another round, the male took charge and ordered them both to run. "Go, go, go!" he cried. "Run, and don't look back!"

Her reply was another scream, this time wobbling from her

throat. The deputy surmised she was following instructions, tearing through the brush at a run.

The game warden was bent forward, his hands on his knees, the gun dangling there as he choked with laughter. The deputy watched the man carefully and, when he had stopped hacking, he asked if they could just get back to the party.

"I reckon you might need a Scotch," the game warden said.

"I'm sure of it," the deputy said. Until the *troubles*, as he thought of the incident at the *Tribune*, reporting had been the right calling for him. He had admitted to himself, when his uncle pitched the idea, that this deputy thing would be a sort of lateral move with a bit of a downward twist. But he knew, too, it would be good to get some sun on his back. Flex a muscle or two. Take his 4x4 into some Alabama swampland. Like the song says, he figured he'd just about thought himself into a jail, sitting too long at that computer keyboard. And deputy game warden had sounded good, had all the makings of a boots-and-jeans getaway from the newspaper.

Instead, his new boss was drunk and shooting wildly into the night sky, scaring the bejeezus out of a couple of kids. They were trespassing on private property. The pay was low. The uniform pants were an inch too long. He had other uncles. Maybe they had better ideas.

A SOUTHERLY WIND ROSE UP IN THE BACKWATER MARSHES off Weeks Bay a quarter mile from the widow's cottage and bent the tall grasses and rippled the black water, like some unseen hand stirring through things out there. A great blue heron paused with one long stick-skinny leg bent, its lizard-like toes curled into a clawed fist and frozen a foot above the brackish water.

Perhaps annoyed, the haughty bird cocked its head and blinked a citrine eye in the direction of some little racket, a footfall on a dry stick as a man crept quietly toward Ghost-head Oak. The veteran had heard the gunshot, and wondered if some late-night whiskey had burned more than a throat. He moved toward the tree carefully, quietly. The heron soon enough quit the distraction and once again fished for a crab or a minnow, maybe a snake.

In his peripheral vision, the veteran caught a shadow moving in the sky. A crow blacker than the night that held the moon cupped its quiet wings against the wind and descended late for her roost. He wondered what had kept the bird from sleep. Someone else might have missed it, but from this distance his soldier's eye could see the crow settle on a topmost branch of Ghosthead Oak. Then he lost sight of the bird in the tree's silhouette, yet heard a flutter and guessed it shook its satiny feathers as it found balance for sleeping.

The veteran twitched and instinctively dropped into a crouch when a low feline grumble, some wildcat on a feeding prowl raised a complaint nearby.

He spoke to the cat: "You don't like all the monkey-fight business either?"

The veteran sneaked through the same stand of grass, where forty-some years earlier on a certain night and during another full moon he had silently navigated the night. That night a screen door had banged open, rasping back on rusty hinges and slamming against unpainted clapboards warped and loosened by seasons of hurricanes, a ruckus raised with enough volume to throb past Ghosthead Oak, only fading finally to silence somewhere downriver. He was a boy of seventeen or so when he had been shoved forward through the open door onto the porch. He had on no shirt and was barefoot and his hands were tied behind his back with a frayed scrap of dock line, so he could not break his fall with his arms.

The episode of anger had bloomed, as so often happened, from soil gentle enough. The boy's father worked for

Baldwin Farms and had just finished up a week of dawn-to-dusk days getting in the potato crop. Every one of those hot August nights he had dragged home a sunburned dirty neck and a sweat-sopped collar and the temper of a cornered blue crab. His best nights were those when he would sink deeply into his favorite diversion, the week's episode of *Gunsmoke*.

James Arness, Marshal Matt Dillon, was the reason there was a television in the room. In its solid cherry case it was the prettiest piece of furniture in the whole house. When, after five years, the TV show changed from a half hour to an hour-long program, you would have thought the Lord Jesus Christ was scheduled to stop by their house for a visit Saturday nights at 10 p.m. Nights when the boy's uncle would come to watch were best, so welcome was the man's easy laughter and eyes full of grace that even his father sat looser on the couch.

Into the show's second decade, when the black-and-white images took on living color, the whole of Heaven might have descended on the swampy landscape along the east banks of Fish River when the Sears Silvertone was delivered, set up, and angled into the corner of the front room. The boy did not know another family with a color television.

Nor did the boy know another family that so easily spilled into its own drama.

When the landlord stopped by to give notice of a raise in the next month's rent, he watched his father that night move their furniture into the yard, douse the old house with diesel fuel, and gaze at the walls and roof as they disappeared, watched him burn to a pile of black ashes the sagging four-room hovel. His father, eyes red from heat, swallowing beer, tossed his bottle onto the smoldering heap.

His mother had said nothing, would not take her husband to task for some bizarre act, for such was the way of madmen. And this man, her husband, when he was riled, his rage was bigger than a blue thunderhead, meaner than a coiled moccasin. The boy had heard his father brag that there was not a thick-necked man in all of Baldwin County, Alabama, drunk or sober, who'd test battle skills with him.

Nor did the boy doubt it that night when the silence in the small living room had closed back in on his question. "Mama, did you know this *Frankenstein* book was written by a lady? I wonder that a woman could make up such a monster. It sure is a scary thing."

His mother had said, "I expect so."

She had turned a page, not even looking up from her magazine, and the boy knew she'd hardly heard what he'd said. He had not spoken loudly, since his chair was near hers. Only a small round mahogany table separated them, and they shared the yellow light from a tall lamp. His uncle had made it from a varnished cypress knee, and it sat on a white lace doily at the center of the table.

His father sat where he always did, in the center of a worn and lumpy couch. He leaned forward to flick ashes from his Chesterfield's into an empty Budweiser bottle, leaned forward to catch every word from Miss Kitty and Doc and the marshal, leaned forward to get ahead of the life curling in behind him.

The boy had been surprised when the commercial came on and his father turned his head toward him and ordered, "Come here, boy, and let me see if I can tie that knot the marshal just used on the outlaw."

The boy closed his book, shot a nervous look at his mother, then got up and walked barefoot to the couch. His mother watched him, folding shut the magazine but not moving in her chair.

"Turn around and put your hands behind your back," the father said, twirling the end of a scrap of dock line that he had been half-heartedly eye-splicing during the commercials.

The boy hadn't much time to wonder where this was going before he felt the rope cut into his wrists, and knew his father had made fast the marshal's knot, or some version of it. Then he felt the flat of his father's big hand on his back. The boy grunted when the blow came from the heel of his father's palm. The loud voice sounded poured through rusted nails and broken glass when he growled that he was not going to be found guilty of raising *no such a boy as you.*

"I figure if I put you out in the dark," the father said, "run you out of the house and chase you down by the river, leave you there until the sun comes up, I reckon, by God, you'll know that nothing in God's world is like that shit you read in those books. If something's going to bite you, it'll be some alligator or a snake. A wildcat might scratch you. But you'll not encounter no damn slobbering full-moon werewolves. You hear me, son? A bullet or a bare-knuckled fist is the only monster you'll ever run up against."

The boy's mother finally pounded her fist on the chair arm and said, "Damn you!"

She jumped to her feet and rushed at him. He waited until she was near and jabbed his extended finger so hard into her chest that she stumbled backwards toward her chair, and sat down hard there. Before she could rise, he had clamped his great paw around the boy's neck and shoved him out of the living room, through the kitchen, toward the screened back door.

The boy was booted in the small of his back, so that he fell headlong into the doorjamb, twisted and caught the screen door with his shoulder and fell onto the porch. He thudded onto the cypress-planked floor, turning his head so he would not smash his nose, but he somehow did anyway, and it ran blood and mucous. When the man who followed snatched him up from the boards with a handful of blond hair, thick and curly, a red knot had ballooned beneath an abrasion on the boy's right cheek. A raised nail head snagged his left shoulder and blood poured down the boy's brown-skinned arm.

Now he was on his feet and licking at the blood running

onto his upper lip. He quickly turned to face his father, glancing past him to where his mother stood weeping behind the screen door, her hands in fists at her mouth.

"If your head was not stuck so deep in some book or the other," the father told his son, "you'd know about real things of the night. You'd be ready for the mission I'm sending you on."

He adjusted his stance to brace for another shove, widened his feet, lowered his head and shoulders and bunched the muscles in his legs and torso. His father had only raised his arm, pointed his finger into the night, and said, "Get out of here. Get away from this house, boy."

He heard his mother say, but softly, "Son."

His father told her to shut up.

"You stay gone until morning, boy. Keep off the highway. Stay in the woods. Learn a lesson about the night. And when you come home, leave your panties in the swamp. I'll hang some men's drawers on your bedpost. You'll be surprised how easy they wear. Hell, you might even grow up to be man enough to get in the U.S. Army."

On a thousand other nights, at least that many, he had gone to the tree. Sometimes under a sky that was so black that all sound was vexed to silence, and sometimes under a sky filigreed with nameless stars or brushed with the moon's soft silver patina. His books were a delight to him, but the tree was a friend. When he climbed onto one of its low-curving massive branches, or leaned bareback against its rough hide, a night could go like a run of good sentences by Mr. William Faulkner. The air and the sounds and the thin scent of fish on the wind had cloaked him like a blanket.

That night, as the boy limped toward Ghosthead Oak, the moon was round as some ancient Mayan pendant, a hard-edged disc of dirty white, scribbled upon with gray shadows that really did make a face, and it frowned on his going through the Spartina marsh, the cord grass getting shorter as the soft ground rose toward the giant tree.

A cool dew fell on him, and his naked arms and shoulders and back were shiny with it. His bare feet, too, felt the wet chill of the ground and it was a comfort to him, tempting his thoughts out of his head and into the nerve endings in his skin.

He knew his mother would not follow. He guessed that she would not sleep at all tonight, that she would breathe shallow, lying open-eyed with her back to his father. In the darkness of their bedroom she would hate her fear, but she would not dare follow her son. If she got out of the bed her husband's derangement would find in her its target for discharge, like low summer lightning ripping through a tall pine.

The boy's arm and face burned with pain and the bloody flow over his lip could only be spat away. He wished for the use of his hands all the more. But the rope was tied up good and tight. Marshal Dillon might have been proud of his father's skill, though the good lawman surely would have drawn his gun against such meanness.

There were sharply drawn moonshadows all about the ground, fallen darkly there like soot from the scrub bushes.

The wind turned from the south and charged to the east, then whipped quickly back before taking an easterly hold. It brushed through the grass, a loud *shishhh* in the gusts. The boy walked with greater determination, anxious to bring the great oak into view. The breeze calmed and in the lull he heard an alligator, a small quick one, splashing through the Juncus toward the open water of the river.

The narrow, winding path to the tree was the same pathway the boy had always used, a looping, lazy arc toward the riverbank and along it for a ways before a break in the waving run of tall cattails allowed a view inland of the mammoth live oak shouldering up the sky from its grassy hummock.

After the water's edge, back of a broad savannah of needlerush with its five-foot-tall, grayish green stemlike blades, the live oak stood in silhouette against the treeline of the high ground. Pines and tupelo gums and magnolias, maples and bayberries grew together thickly and made a billowing perimeter behind the tree that was set back a good quarter mile in the manner, perhaps, of respectful subjects.

Now the boy had come abreast of the cattails and knew he did not have far to go. The moonlight, when he centered his awareness on the odd silver cast illuminating this dead-of-night sojourn, eased the pain in his jaw and shoulder, the throb in his head.

There were other things a boy could count on. The moon in its loop around the earth did not equivocate in its rhythm, kept hard to its promise to lay out a year's worth of months. Tonight it was at the top of its cycle, waxing as round and bright as its August turn would allow.

He could count on Ghosthead Oak.

He knew as sure as the man in the moon where he was bound, that he would spend the night cradled in a bough of that tree. Safe, then, he knew that nothing bumping about in the night would unhinge his ease.

The boy's uncle found him in the morning and the boy did not even attempt to get up from sitting against the tree. He waited. His hands and wrists hurt behind his back. Places on him ached and burned. The blood from the nail snag had dried brown on his arm.

"Your mama told me I might find you here."

The uncle stopped on the perimeter of the big tree's cool shade and looked at the boy. "She told me what he did."

The boy's uncle was as even-keeled as any man the boy had ever known, and he watched to see how this would read on his uncle's face.

But what he saw gave him no confidence that this squall would just blow over.

Out of the morning sun, underneath Ghosthead Oak's canopy, staring too long at the boy, the uncle said, "I'll kill him for this." He said it slowly, with the certain conviction that would accompany the giving of his name to a stranger.

A cold shudder seized the boy, but passed, and reformed in his brain as an icy clot of worry about what would now pass between them.

"Daddy was just drinking," the boy offered.

"Nothing to say to me. Not anymore," the uncle said. "Clear to me what has to be done, as clear as those bruises you carry."

He told the boy to turn around as he fished a folding knife from his pocket. He knelt, muttering curses as he sawed the blade back and forth. The ropes fell onto the ground at the boy's heels. His uncle put his hand on his shoulder.

"You could have walked the path to my place."

The boy said nothing. Then, "The tree was a good place to come."

"You're mighty calm, but you can't keep me out of this, boy. My sister cannot. God in Heaven cannot." The uncle turned, said, "Come with me."

They walked on, dodging tree branches and side-stepping blackberry briars. The boy saw a garter snake slither into the brush. Last night's clouds had all given way to the morning sun, and it shone off dark green leaves sprouting thick in this understory vegetation.

At the uncle's place, he cleaned and dressed the scrapes and cuts, put ointment on the boy's wrist. When the first aid was finished, his uncle washed up at the small sink and wiped his hands on a worn-out dishtowel taken from its hook near the window beside the kitchen sink.

His uncle tossed the rag onto the counter, said, "Bastard. Sorry bastard."

He put his hand on the boy's shoulder, then placed a finger underneath his chin and lifted his face. The boy locked eyes with the man. The boy had never seen a man cry, and not this time either, but a deep reddening wetness did come to his uncle's eyes.

"I am sorry," he said to the boy, "that I have waited so long to straighten things out. Back there, there's a clean t-shirt for you. Now you get dressed, and stay down here. There's some biscuits in the oven, and a plate with bacon. Some fresh eggs and your mama's strawberry jam in the refrigerator. You have yourself something to eat. Don't you come out of this house, you hear?"

His uncle fetched from a cupboard in the tiny bedroom his Smith & Wesson revolver, a walnut-handled, nickel-plated .38-caliber with a four-inch barrel.

"What're you going to do?" the boy asked.

The man did not answer, only took cartridges from a coffee can on a shelf at the top of his closet and loaded the chamber. He pitched a t-shirt to the boy and went to the front door, opened it without haste, and stepped outside. The boy sprang up and dashed out of the trailer. He fell into step behind his uncle, who was now hurrying up the path toward the highway. They walked past his uncle's rusty red GMC pickup, and the boy knew his uncle was walking off some anger. That might help.

"I told you," his uncle said, his brown eyes straight ahead, his footfalls steady, "to stay put, son."

"No."

"Just as well, then. Your daddy'll be home for lunch. And he's about to get a taste of something he didn't expect."

The two of them went not far down the road, the boy three steps behind the man, to a driveway of sun-baked brown dirt. They turned and went up a low hill toward the front yard of the boy's house. The boy now had to trot along to keep up, sweating, the back and chest of the clean t-shirt his uncle had tossed to him wet clear through.

"Mama," the boy yelled, "he's got a gun! He's after Daddy!"

"Shut up," his uncle commanded.

His father came to the front door and opened it with a grin, cutting his eyes back over his shoulder into the dim recess of the living room, maybe looking for his wife.

"Say what, boy?" the father said, hardly taking notice of his brother-in-law, and looked again behind himself.

"You rotten bastard," said the boy's uncle. The grin fell off his father's face, now seeing the gun, its barrel aimed at him and he lifted his hands as if to hold back his assailant.

"Whoa, boy. Just hang on there."

"You got three minutes to get in your car and be on the highway, leaving this place. You'll never lay a hand on this boy or his mother again. Ever. Go and don't come back."

The boy watched the two men locked in a stare, and he could not breathe. He wished now he'd stayed down the hill as he'd been told. His father wiped his mouth on his bare forearm, as if this action might buy him enough time to formulate a plan.

"That boy come and get you? Tell you he was scared of the dark?"

"Now you got two and a half minutes."

The boy's uncle cocked the hammer and stepped aside as if to let his brother-in-law pass. He stepped in place, telegraphing his impatience. The boy didn't believe that his uncle intended to grant his father time even for shoes, a change of shirt and pants, or his wallet. This countdown was nonnegotiable.

"Now you've got two minutes till your free ride to the funeral home."

The fat shiny pistol was steady in his uncle's fist, his arm extended straight out.

"You gotta let me get on a shirt and my boots."

"No I don't."

Then the boy's uncle fired a round into the boards of the porch, busting up splinters not six inches from his father's right foot, who sprang so high it looked like the slapstick acts the boy had seen on *The Ed Sullivan Show*. His father stumbled and banged his shoulder on the doorjamb.

"You crazy bastard," the boy's father croaked.

"Yes, I am. Crazy for waiting until I found your son with his hands tied to deal with you."

The boy's uncle raised the pistol to eye level and cupped

his left hand under the right to steady his aim. He drew a bead on his brother-in-law.

When the boy whimpered his uncle told him once more to shut up. Though firmly spoken, the words were an instruction that lacked anger, only carried unflinching authority.

His uncle cocked the hammer again. The click locked down time for the boy.

His father danced back inside the house, quick-footed, and in ten seconds had snagged a shirt and his boots, but hadn't had enough time to put them on. He bounded out the door, across the porch past his son and his brother, fishing out his car keys as he ran across the yard.

The boy's father whipped around to the driver's side door of his Olds, opened the door, and with one foot on the threshold plate, yelled, "I ain't some nigger you just run off the farm. You better watch. When you least expect it—"

While the words still hung in the air, their slight vibration was split like dry white oak stove wood by an explosion from the pistol. And then a hollow stillness.

The boy waited round-eyed for his father to fall backwards. Instead, he jumped straight up and hollered, plenty alive.

"The next one," his uncle said, "goes in your right eye socket."

The boy's mother came running around the corner of the house with a basket of fresh-picked green beans just in time to see, in a well-greased motion, her husband slide into his car. She watched bewildered as he spun the engine to life, jerked the shift lever to drive, and gunned it, scratching loose a plume of brown dirt. The Oldsmobile's whitewalls squalled as the car fishtailed onto Pensacola highway eastbound. A faint odor of scalded rubber drifted over the yard and floated on gray dust.

No one moved, or spoke.

Their eyes watched the dust cloud spin away, as it grew thinner and soared over the housetop, above the ragged tree line back of the house. The boy's mind gauged the void, the silence thumping in his ears.

Now, these forty-some years later, the noise of gunfire at the tree drew him toward its shadow, wondering at the unnatural violation of the night in its branches.

THE SUN ROSE ON A COLD MORNING, JUST DAYS SHY OF Christmas. The trespassers were gone home. The widow pulled on a denim jacket and went behind her house to a shed leaning there beneath a tall pine and an old crepe myrtle, its bare branches scratching at the tin roof and shiplap siding.

She tugged hard on the door, pulling it free of the dirt and moss that wanted to reclaim the bottom boards. Gray light from the open door made a slanted rectangle on the floor and softened the dim interior. From the corner, hanging there on a galvanized hook, she took an empty six-foot-long cotton-picking sack, itself a remnant of other hands who had tended the same soil beneath her feet. She folded it across her shoulder, and the tail of it dragged across the yard as she went along the ruts of an abandoned road a little ways to the edge of the grassy field.

At the fencerow, the widow paused to straighten the weathered tin sign that begged NO TRESPASSING. She had put the sign there—how long ago now? Just some weeks after her father died. She had driven a single fat 16-penny nail through its center and into the post. The sign turned on that axis, sometimes owing to the wind, but mostly on account of this one and that one twisting it. Sometimes when she went out there in the morning the words were upside down.

Or turned sideways.

Or, as today, tilted like a ship sinking.

She adjusted the sign and set the words on the level.

Then she walked north along the fencerow for twenty yards. She went sure-footed through waist-high grass that still flashed some green, a winter privilege for most plants in these coastal parts of Alabama. She found the break in the fence where a gate had once swung on noisy hinges. She went through the opening, as none of the trespassers ever did. Their coming and going had beat down a footpath that made a shortcut right over the barbed wire fence. She wondered why they never went those few steps farther to the proper entrance.

The widow angled back through the weeds and took up the hard-packed trail of the trespassers to the base of Ghosthead Oak. She drew quietly beneath its low-swaying thick branches, into that chilly shade some two hundred feet across. She was keen to do this little task at Ghosthead Oak, pick up what-have-you from last night's intruders. The terrified screams from the girl and her young man, and the silly hoot and gasping laughter that followed had broken something like fine crystal in her head. She just wanted to get this cleanup chore over with.

She paused and looked at the mess. Then she bent and picked up the beer cans and bottles and cigarette butts. She used a long stick to pick up the leavings of fumbled sex, turning her head as she dropped such into the sack. She gathered the hamburger wrappers and other food cartons and cups.

What she had collected was not heavy, the product of just more than a week's traffic. She looked to make sure she'd picked up all the trash and wondered that she had not found spent shell casings from the gunshot. She put her hand to her forehead and noticed for the first time deep scratches or cuts on an exposed root where it twisted free of the soil like a subterranean serpent.

She let go the cotton sack and walked over to the tree. She crouched on one knee and rubbed her hand over the torn bark, recognizing the marks left by a huge wildcat that had sharpened its claws. Most likely, this was the work of the same cat she'd heard yowling many times on her land since just before Thanksgiving. Had it now staked a claim on Ghosthead Oak? A chill spread across her back and goose bumps peppered her arms, though a bobcat should never present a real threat to her. Like all the wild animals in the swamps, it preferred to stay far clear of humans. Only a mother cat with her young would be extremely aggressive. Even with what she knew of a bobcat's habits, the widow wished at this moment for her dog to be more of the faithful at-her-side variety than the capricious companion it was.

The widow picked up the top of the cotton sack, this time looping its long strap over her shoulders and letting her load drag the ground as a fieldhand might have. Once, while crossing the fence, between bottles and cans rattling around in the sack, she thought she heard the brief squall of a wildcat in the distance toward Weeks Bay, but that was not at all likely, she decided. Bobcats were nocturnal hunters and would never be out on business in broad daylight. They worked only in the low light of dusk and dawn.

When she arrived at her cottage, her black dog lay on the porch. It yawned, stretched, and stood up, then bounded down and walked over to her, tail wagging, for a pat on the head. For a moment the widow just stood and looked at the dog, its amber eyes fixed on hers. The dog stopped swinging its tail from side to side, and sat down, muzzle raised, waiting. The widow shook her head and stroked the fur between the dog's ears.

When she went on around the corner of the house, the dog followed. She took a plastic lighter from her jacket pocket and set fire to paper and cardboard inside a rusting metal, dented fifty-five-gallon drum. She reached for broken twigs and kindling and tossed them into the fire, then larger sticks until the fire was a busy yellow blaze. She pitched in the rubble and detritus from the bottom of her sack.

From out of nowhere a thought dropped into her head,

landing there like a bird shot on the wing, and she was appalled when it raised its head, fixing her with the urge to just set fire to the tree. Soak the base in kerosene and throw a match.

Shame immediately smothered her breathing, and she crossed herself like Spanish women did in movies, a gesture completely foreign to the Baptist raising she got at her mother's hand. But more bizarre was this impulse to torch Ghosthead Oak. When the thin aluminum cans began to melt and the first of the beer bottles burst in a *pop!* of shattering glass, she went inside. Her black dog followed on her heels and she closed the door against the day, shutting out tree and trespassers alike. For a long spell she sat in front of the hearth clinging to her lap blanket.

SHE DID NOT KNOW, WHEN SHE HAD CHOSEN HIM, THAT the goat herder had once been a lawyer. Nor did she know she would be his widow before she turned forty. She only knew that he had beautiful arms.

She had turned off the highway and driven to his small farm because a neat hand-lettered sign on the roadside, partly obscured by a big palmetto palm, proclaimed: FRESH GOAT CHEESE AND HONEY AT THE END OF THE LANE. She was curious.

Plus, her father loved raw honey, relished chewing the waxy comb until he had swallowed all its sweetness. Ironic that the gift of a jar of honey for him would lead her off the family place and out of her father's house. An irony, too, that such would bring her to know as never before how it had been for him after her mother passed.

She was a beautiful woman, her hair heavy and curving and shining black. Her eyes were light hazel, almost gray, her nose and lips perfectly formed according to some universal prescription that stirred men's fancy.

And some women.

They whispered and nodded that she must be "sweet on the girls" since she had gone off up North to college and had come home to Magnolia Springs without a man. Nor did she take up dating and that was their proof.

Men who saw her could only stare in silence and wonder what it would be like to be chosen by this beauty who was as tall as most of them, whose body could have been a pattern-mold for high fashion mannequins, whose tanned skin was brushed with faint freckles as smooth as a child's, though she was maybe thirty.

On that day, at the end of the lane, she had said *excuse me* to the man beside the fence when he kept about feeding his goats for some minutes while she stood there. The leafy cut branches he let them nibble from his hand had the goats wide-eyed and tense, each anxious to get its full share. She was unaware how the process of buying honey or cheese at this place was to be conducted, but she could discern rude behavior, and this man's was exemplary.

Even after she spoke to him, the goat herder would not look at her, nor did he until he had fended off the stubborn billy that wanted to head-butt his mixed-breed Labrador-something between mouthfuls of greenery. He called *Joe* in a commanding voice, trying to tempt the shiny black dog out of harm's way in the goat pen.

His frayed white cotton shirtsleeves were rolled up past

his elbows and the fine curly hairs on his arms—long like a basketball player's—caught the late afternoon sun and drew her eye to the subtle veins raised along his muscled forearms, down to his strong wrists and wide hands, to the same golden hairs on his knuckles, and to his fingers made for playing a piano.

Or caressing the small of her back. She decided, when he finally focused his brown eyes on her, that this man at the end of the lane was the man she would marry.

And when they had been married for ten years, he could still hold her with his gaze in such a way that her breathing seemed charged with some drug, a narcotic that focused all her attention on his face. When he looked at her and smiled, she felt as though she were being physically pulled toward him.

She also learned to work beside him—she fed the goats, made cheese, robbed honey from the bees. She moved in work with him like they were dancers. She let him lead and followed several steps behind as they each carried a kid goat, hauling the small creatures to safety. They were slogging across the edge of a shallow slough that pooled rising floodwaters, muddy, spinning leaves and debris around their calves. The season's first hurricane was coming ashore thirty miles south near Orange Beach.

"This storm would be much scarier if it were dark out. I'm glad for the daylight at least," she said, raising her voice above the wind.

She thought her husband might turn and tell her not to worry when he pitched forward without making a sound. The young goat bleated as it toppled from his long arms and landed splay-legged upon the soft, rain-slick ground and scrambled into the brush. She threw the goat aside and fell beside her husband to turn him over, get his face out of the puddle he'd fallen into.

She turned him over and his eyes were closed and he was not moving. She could feel, as surely as if she had seen it go from him, that his life was gone.

And the storm winds ripped across the pasture and tore into the perimeter trees where its drone muted her cries and blew the hard rain into her face and, there on her knees, she could not feel her own tears.

IF YOU GO OUT THERE TO THE WIDOW'S PLACE," THE GAME warden said to the deputy, "then you need to add in a little work stuff."

"I was going after work today," he responded. "On my own time."

The deputy stood at the status board, spraying down the glossy white write-on wipe-off surface with cleaner to clear away the smudges and ghost writing. Otherwise, there was no status of any issue to report or track there. He wiped the splotches as the liquid ran down the board. It wasn't working to erase the darkest lettering. As the other smudges came clean, words dimly legible were revealed. They said, PANTHER MY ASS.

"You don't have any time, son, that's just yours. Don't you know the nature of public service. You are on call twenty-four, seven."

"I know I'm on call as needs arise…"

"As I say is when you're on call. To hell with *need*," the

game warden said.

"Okay. Okay," the deputy said. "What duties are in order for me if I go to the widow's place?"

"You have to tell her a story."

"What the hell? A story? Are you kidding?"

"I'm known as lots of things in this county," said the game warden. "A 'kidder' I ain't heard yet."

"Alright, what story do I tell the woman? And what's the story behind, 'Panther my ass'? Did you write that here?"

"I wrote it. I erased it. Doesn't want to come off good, though."

"Why'd you write it?"

"Miss Loo down at the bait shop has this coffee klatch," the game warden said, getting up from his desk to walk to the window. He looked in silence toward the parking lot and scrub pines. In a moment, almost as if remembering his place, he said, "A bunch of old coots and loons. One of 'em, this old Captain MacNee fellow, told the dead peckers at the bait shop he saw a black panther running the bank of the river. Not skittish at all. Just loping along casting a look sideways at him now and again."

"Wow!"

"What the hell do you mean, 'wow'? There ain't been a panther in these parts in a hundred years. Unless it rolled in with the circus."

"You know I heard something about the return of black panthers to Florida swamps," the deputy said, excited. "I could probably get a friend to check the *Tribune's* archives."

"Come here, son."

The deputy joined the game warden at the window, his wiping cloth wadded in his hand.

"Two things: One, see that tag on my truck?"

"Yes."

"Can you make out what state it indicates?"

"Alabama."

"Not Florida?"

"Not Florida."

"Then why the hell would I care what a bunch of Florida Geographic types have got to say about my jurisdiction?"

"Well…"

"Second: The official word from a bunch of Florida wildlife sanctuary nerds is, and I quote, 'For years there have been stories of black panthers prowling the woods and swamps of Florida's wilderness, but there is no official record they exist.' Look it up, son. But not on my time."

"I will. But nobody doubts Florida cougars, you know."

"Third: I wrote that up there on the board when Miss Loo at the baitshop put up a reward poster for a picture of a black panther. Or information leading to a sighting. What the hell kind of crap stories is that going to generate? A Florida Fish and Wildlife officer got called out in the middle of the night by some panicky woman. Her black panther turned out to be a dark bobcat. You think I want every fruitcake nature lover calling me off on wild goose chases?"

"You mean wild cat chases?" the deputy asked with a smile.

"Smart ass crap'll get you no place around here," the game warden said. He continued, "Four:…"

"You said two things."

"Four: Here's the story you tell the widow—you tell her I said I've got a crazy cousin in Mississippi, a holdover Civil War reject reenactor, a drunk and a fool."

The deputy nodded, fighting back a grin.

"You tell her he learned one of our kin was lynched in the dark days following the War of Yankee Aggression, accused of stealing cattle. Mob rule turned mean and they hung him. You tell her my cousin is on a mission, ordained by the Lord in his mind, to burn down every hanging tree left standing in the known South. He's hit three so far without getting caught."

"You should turn him in," the deputy said, stepping away from the window.

"He's kin. The Lord is on his side," the game warden declared. "You tell the widow there is a myth of a hanging that took place at Ghosthead Oak in the middle of the last century. You tell her I have not told my cousin that story because I am a good friend to big trees."

"You're serious?" the deputy asked, his eyebrows high.

"Now that's one I've heard: 'That game warden, he's a serious man.' Yes, sir. That one fits."

THE VETERAN HATED THE WAR LONG BEFORE HE BECAME a brown water sailor and set foot on the thirty-one-foot deck of a PBR in the Song Ong Doc River. There were other rivers with odd-sounding names, their banks scattered with river patrol boats left behind as they were caught in ambushes and damaged beyond use.

On the river, it was point-on: deny the Viet Cong use of the Mekong Delta waterways. Period. The four-man PBRs saw almost continuous bloody action. Almost three thousand sailors died in coastal and river operations. One died in his lap.

He did not like his job, the big bosses half a world away sipping coffee in Washington offices.

He liked the boats. Jacuzzi jet-drive twin diesels with fiberglass hulls that could turn almost in their own length. Go like a bat out of hell, or reverse the drives and stop in seconds. The PBRs drew only two feet of water and were the right vessel on the shallow, weed-choked rivers, but he did sometimes wish for more than the twin .50-caliber machine guns.

He liked the men he served with in country. Every one of them. Sergeants and lieutenants alike.

He did not like college. His grades confirmed it. When four Fs and an X overwrote his student deferment at the end of his fourth semester at the University of Alabama, he knew it was time to give up pitchers of beer at The Chukker and make a plan. He would get a draft notice in short order.

His maternal uncle, a decorated veteran of WWII had told him the worst rolling deck in the South China Sea was better than the warmest foxhole in Viet Nam, and he'd believed him. This uncle shot straight with him in all matters from fishing the backwaters to French kissing. This uncle had drawn a pistol bead on his father, cleared his life of a world of shit. So he called the Navy recruiter and asked where to sign.

No way he could've known he would not draw a berth on a fat carrier in the North Atlantic. What were the odds it would have gone down the way it did? That his sailor's deck would not roll across the sea, but slingshot down muddy rivers. He wondered if he would have hit the books harder and come up with good grades like his roommate if he'd known what work he was setting for his hands, where he'd be taking his eyes. What man would ask his eyes to blink in such an alien place, let particles of hell stream in?

What woman could sleep beside a man growling and

yelping through dreams?

Forty years later, he sat in his banged-up Airstream trailer on his little piece of the backside-of-nowhere he'd bought on Fish River. The property's waterfront boundary was marshy wetlands and unbuildable by local codes. Alright by him.

Nobody came here. No ex-wives. No children.

Good by him.

These were the same woods the veteran had once barefooted through with a cane pole slung over his shoulder and a bucket swinging from his hand. Used to climb the big oak tree down the river a ways. More than once he fell asleep in the cozy lap where its main branches parted. He had once slept with his hands tied behind him and his bare back against its rough bark. He had felt more secure sleeping at the tree than in his own narrow bedroom. Even after his father left.

But that was a long time ago, and he'd had no reason to come back once his mother had left a shady spot a half-mile away. When she hired the transporters to drag the Frontier single-wide down to the corner of a bean field in Foley, he let a piece of his mind go numb to the sense of place. Which held until he got to Southeast Asia and his heart drove home to Alabama every night.

But when he put on his civilian shoes, he walked them into bars, bobbing and weaving to avoid stillness. It took the veteran twenty-five years to finally take a good long look at his grades, posted on the bottom of the top bunk in a jail cell in Pensacola. This time, he didn't need any advice.

With fallow-lying money his father had willed to him, and the interest it earned while he refused to remove it from the bank, he paid cash for a deed to 4.97 acres and an Airstream trailer, same vintage as his first year in the Navy. He'd dragged his shiny trailer to the end of River Road within a mile of the land where he and his mother lived, through a copse of poplar and bay and a few limber willows and parked it on the hump of high ground back of the run of swamp. This was his own quiet preserve of dinosaur habitat, and even though those rough beasts were gone now, arm-thick moccasins and jack-jawing birds he couldn't name were suitable replacements for those mythic reptiles.

Living on the river, the veteran had fished for most of his first three months while he waited for a job with the post office that never came. While he ate several meals of fried mullet he caught in the water beneath his dock and cheese grits with onions he grew in his backyard, he hit upon his retirement plan: that he would take it now. *Thanks, Daddy.*

From the highground where the Airstream sat, down the slope, across a long and lazy board bridge through the wetlands, the veteran's piece of ground had two hundred feet fronting Fish River. There he'd built of five-quarter rough-sawn cypress a dockhouse the size of a room. No walls, only four fat pilings driven into the mud at the bottom of the river, great long poles that extended upward to support an open floor, about six feet off the water, and a green-shingled hip roof. Six additional, shorter pilings created two boat slips. In one was moored the veteran's wooden skiff.

His fishing nets and hooks and lines and rods and reels, and all manner of boating gear, were stowed here and there at the little dockhouse: cane poles overhead in the rafters, nets hanging on nails and hooks, paddles and gaffs and gigs standing in two corners in open-top wooden kegs, two small outboard motors clamped to a section of handrail, a wide board shelf holding two gasoline cans and a portable fuel tank and hose, the whole inventory in admirable order for the quantity and array of it all.

Facing the slow swirl and run of the river on its approach to Weeks Bay, the veteran watched the jumping mullet and tail-flipping gars. From two Adirondack chairs painted pure white with their high, leaning backs he presided over it all, in parade review of the gliding pelicans and seagulls.

He had cut back some saplings so he could at least get a narrow view of the river. His back stayed slick with sweat during that good work, and his muscles, when he reached the ax high over his head and pulled it down into a tree trunk with a twist of his torso, they rolled and flexed like machine parts under his skin and his one tattoo shone blue on his bicep: USN in block letters an inch tall.

The veteran put up his feet on the dinette tabletop and listened to the darkness. Caught an owl's query as he sipped Jack Daniels. Something crashing in the palmetto bushes at the edge of the marsh. A mosquito buzzed, loose and on the prowl somewhere in his cherrywood cocoon.

He leaned over, pushed his loose-hanging blond and gray hair from his eyes and slipped a CD into his player. He chose a track, then eased up the volume on Brandi Carlisle singing Cohen's *Hallelujah*. He closed his eyes. When the singer told that love's not a victory march, said that it's a cold and it's a broken hallelujah, he cried. And set down the whiskey. He had not been drunk in nine years.

The weepy crap, as the veteran thought of it, he attributed in some measure to drink, and both in larger measure to fighting a schizophrenic war forty years ago. And his daddy still.

The veteran's memories of those two years in country sprang up like deranged, bus-flattened cartoon characters to do their freaky horror show in his dreams. And yet on the front bumper of the veteran's Toyota Hi-Lux pickup was a tag silk-screened in the likeness of his Viet Nam service ribbon, yellow with green stripes at either end and three red ones in the middle. Flying the colors was a contradiction of war. Irreconcilable. Like the disparate natures of the two men who figured strongest in his history. Soldiers both. Heroes of different battlefields in the same war. For not joining up right out of high school his father had called him a pussy. His uncle had told him to run full-tilt to Canada. A cable, bar-tight and humming, was strung between the two men.

The veteran kept both men's photos in the same double

frame, and he poured another shot of Tennessee sour mash and lit another Camel filter and looked at them both. The men stared back at him, each from underneath the bill of his US Army service dress cap. Daddy on the left, uncle to the right. War ribbons and service medals lined above each man's shirt pocket flap, starched, flat-ironed and hard-buttoned.

The veteran sipped Jack Daniels from a tumbler in the square shape of the bottom of the bottle from which it was poured. The glass and a matching tumbler and a bottle of the good stuff came together in a commemorative gift set. His aunt didn't argue with him that day, so many days after the funeral, when he had selected from his father's things this gift box of whiskey.

"I just wonder why he didn't drink it up," she said. "The way that man poured it down."

He knew why the bottle was unopened. No big deal came along in his life worth cracking the seal of such precious liquor. It still remained unopened. For now. The whiskey glass he used each night for one drink.

And the shoes. He'd taken his father's shoes from beneath the edge of the sagging bed the old man died in. Nobody noticed.

He had plenty from his father. Enough to last.

The widow's dog, a bossy and inquisitive female, a scion of old joe, followed her, nudging her thighs. The long-legged, gangly dog wanted to lead the way, and darted past the widow and walked just in front, perking her ears and tossing looks over her shoulders this way or that with her fine broad head.

Her thick tail swept side to side as if she gloated over winning head of the pack. Her coat was splattered with gray mud from the swamp where she liked to romp and explore. Without warning she stopped and the widow bumped into her. The widow patted the dog's rump, which made her spin around on the path.

"Oh, go on there, girl. We've got work this morning. I ordered bees from Australia and they've arrived at the feed and seed store. We'll check the hives and then ride into town."

When her husband died and the sister-in-law from Chicago had showed up asking to buy the place, the widow named a price that was met and within the week she simply moved her things back to her father's house. She had wanted to also move the beehives, which the sister-in-law begged her to do. She hired two men to relocate the bees and watched them close the bees inside the hives at twilight, using mesh to cover their escape slot, and was satisfied they'd transport the bees to a clearing on her father's land. But the men, paid in advance, working in darkness on unfamiliar ground had left them at crazy angles, leaning this way and that. The bees seemed okay with their out-of-plumb housing, and her father declined to help her, so that is how the beehives remained. And, still occupied, except for one, which would get new tenants from Australia.

The dog had stopped again and was reluctant to move on, staring ahead.

"Okay, I'll go first then. You missed your chance."

The widow edged past the dog, still on the point. She looked up after stepping over a piece of broken log on the path and noticed her small herd of goats standing on the knoll inside the wire fence to her right. At a glance she knew something was wrong. Half a dozen of the seventeen goats stood stock still in that trance-like state which followed when something chased the herd and terrorized the animals.

"Damn it," she said.

She'd seen this behavior before and each time at least one or two of the zombie goats died within a day. The six goats that stood frozen in their poses stared blankly in her direction, apathetic and unresponsive to their surroundings.

The first time her husband had called her from the kitchen to come out and see traumatized goats she'd become alarmed and asked him what they could do. He'd said there was nothing to be done. Told her that the veterinarian said some goats and sheep came into this world just looking for a chance to "freeze up and die." And a coyote on the prowl or a roaming dog pack gave them their opportunity. No blood need be spilled to kill a goat.

This episode of terror, the widow believed, was the work of the wildcat she'd heard yowling about the farm for more than a week. That, she imagined, had been why her dog was so wired at bedtime, pacing and whining even after she'd come inside for the night. If she'd put two and two together last night, maybe she could have taken down the shotgun and a spotlight and kept the cat away from the herd.

But she tended the goats little, mostly let them run wild, and they had been rambunctious creatures since she'd relocated them to her father's farm. Her father, though he was glad she'd come home, did not like goats, did not like the way they browsed the underbrush, stripping leaves and small branches. He tolerated them for her sake, because he knew they were a connection to her departed husband and she wouldn't feel right to sell them.

"Damn it," she said again and walked more rapidly to the goats. First to the big male, and then to the others who wouldn't move, in turn patting and soothing the goats without response. The rest of the herd scampered away from her. Odd, she thought, how she had suffered a fitful night of broken sleep and bad dreams. Snippets, really, like a poorly edited preview of a movie about her life with her husband, the timeline and story jumbled.

But in the frames she remembered this morning, his goats scampering here and there through scenes, each time in need of his help. And now these descendants of her husband's herd were making this show and she had no idea what to do. Widowed now for twenty years and still she had not evolved into the strong, self-reliant and resourceful pioneer woman she had believed she would be.

Right now, she missed her husband deeply. She wanted him to come and take care of the goats. Take care of her. See to her and lift the loneliness like a veil so that she could see the beautiful world. And him.

The dynamics of her loneliness had at least become predictable. She would go for months when her husband would stay out of her head except when something caused her to remember a specific event from their marriage. Last week the dog had mixed it up with the graybearded billy at the fenceline, and she'd been catapulted back to that morning when she first saw him, the day she fell headlong in love with him. She had stood at the fencerow, her hands on the twisted wire, and let the memory fill her head like a favorite song, a sweet melody.

And sometimes—she could feel these swings coming, feel them in her bones, like her father's arthritic knees warned of changes in the weather—she'd be pulled down into a week of sadness so thick and heavy she thought she'd drown.

A goat standing beside her bleated, shaking the widow from her brown study. She turned her head and froze in fear.

Standing not thirty yards away was a panther. A cat, black and five feet long with a tail thicker than her arm. Not the bobcat she imagined, this cat's head was thick and square with yellow eyes. There suddenly sprang in her mind a crazy association with the melanistic panther of her childhood, Bhageera. But the oddment of nostalgia was ripped away by a bare-fanged snarl from this very real panther. Her dog was now standing at her knee, growling with its hackles raised. The widow had no idea what to do. The panther was on the path between her and home.

The widow's dog, operating now on pure instinct, was entirely certain what should happen next. In a flash of awareness, she knew the dog was about to attack on the run and she bent and snatched its collar and held on with the strength born of an adrenaline flood as her dog stood on its hind legs and barked furiously, wiggling to get free. The panther, regally nonchalant, turned its back and went several steps along the path, then stopped and looked over its shoulder and snarled again. The cat twitched its tail and sprang forward, disappearing into the brush.

The widow sank to her knees and, crying, kissed her dog's head and hugged the dog to her chest until it finally calmed down. Then her own relief transformed into anger.

"Why the hell have you left me here with all this to do?" She bent forward and pounded the ground. Her dog thought there was a game of fetch in the offing and yipped and licked at her fist as it rose and fell.

The widow got up and went for Ghosthead Oak as if toward a drink of water after a day in the desert. She actually thought there might be someone there and she would ask for an escort, maybe even a ride home. She went along in such a hurry that her dog believed she was still of a mind to play, and yipped playfully, darting ahead and turning back, then dashing away again. When a squirrel crossed the path, the dog set up a rumpus like a bloodhound on a convict's trail.

"Just shut up," the widow screamed at her dog, and its head and tail dropped, its brown eyes asking only for forgiveness for the bad thing it had done. When she saw her dog so beaten by the scolding, the widow stopped walking. Her dog sat down, its muzzle almost touching its chest, its eyes rolling upward to seek some sign from the master that all would be well.

"Oh, sweet dog, how you do bring me along."

And the dog stood up immediately, tail wagging.

"So let's go see if there's a trespasser for our little time of need."

The dog was already on the move, heading in just that direction.

THE VETERAN HAD BEEN LISTENING TO THE COMMOTION kept up by the dog, and he heard a story unfold with the change in timbre, pitch and intensity of the barking. It was clear the dog was coming his way. He had strolled to the tree with his new fishing rod, thought to sit there and install the reel and clean and oil it. For a half hour or so he had been leaning against the big tree. Now he had company coming. The veteran mashed out his cigarette, grinding it against the heel of his boot, and dropped the butt into his shirt pocket. He felt a light breeze on his cheek, picked a direction downwind and eased away from the tree into the bushes on the perimeter. He took up a spot next to a huckleberry bush, parked the handle on the ground and held the rod upright beside him, watching, waiting.

He saw first the dog, then the widow. They came under the tree, she casting looks sideways, and over her shoulder, but not toward him. The veteran kept still. He watched the widow about her business, which was to sit in almost the same spot where he'd sat. He even thought she detected he'd been there by the way she looked at the ground beside her then quickly left and right. He was certain he'd left no sign, even to lightly brushing over the leafy indention on the ground where he'd sat. If she had a sense of his presence, it must be her intuition. Which counts, he thought, because he knew such instincts could save a man's life. Or a woman's.

The veteran was surprised at the widow's beauty. So long ago, back in school, she had been the prettiest girl in school. To hear the boys talk, she took the prize. But he knew her to be in her late fifties now and yet she didn't appear over thirty-something. Her skin was smooth and her figure lean. She would set the curve, he thought, at her class reunion, and, with a slight smile, so might he in a different category.

The dog lay down beside the widow's outstretched legs and put its face down between its paws. Suddenly, it lifted its head, and the veteran knew the breeze had freshened and shifted, pushing his scent right to the dog. It jumped up and stood facing his position. Growling, but tentatively. The widow turned toward the brush where he stood, still concealed. He made a decision.

The veteran stepped from the perimeter into the clearing. A man smiling with a fishing rod in his hand should pull the fuse out of this one, he thought. At least it was a better choice than facing down a big black dog in the weeds.

"Excuse me, ma'am. Didn't mean to intrude. I heard

your dog barking and came to check things out."

The widow put a hand down and stood, brushing leaves from her pants. She paused, studying him with a frown. Her face softened as though she recognized him. "You live out there, down by the river."

"Going on three years now. Or is it five? I don't keep up."

"Yes, well, I knew you had bought the place. Matter of fact, we share a property line for a few hundred feet. I don't do much visiting. Your family lived here when you were a boy, but then you moved away."

"Yes, ma'am. I was a grade or two ahead of you in school. We moved in different crowds, I guess you'd say. But talking about losing track, that was more years ago than I can count up."

"A thousand, it seems." She looked at him directly, still studying, he thought. He did not know what to say next.

"I'm sorry to disturb your morning, ma'am. I know you don't like trespassers."

"Excuse me, I…"

"Your sign says so. Pretty straightforward."

"Well, yes. On the other hand, I'm glad you're here. Actually hoped, for a change, there might be someone at the tree. I ran most of the way here. I saw a panther. A black panther on the path from my house. I was afraid to go back that way and…"

"A black panther?"

"Like a mountain lion. That size. Black from nose to tail."

"And it saw you?"

"It snarled at me. I think my dog might have chased him away, though I can't say it ran at all. More like sauntered away."

"Miss Loo down at the bait shop will be glad to hear this. She's got a reward poster on her wall asking for information. I guess you're not the only one to see the cat."

"I'd just as soon you leave me out of it. Please."

"She won't come to interview you."

"She won't, for certain, or even call if you don't tell her what I said. And if you do, soon enough, who knows who will knock at my door, asking for a first-hand account with the panther."

The veteran said nothing. He met her gaze full on.

"I don't do much talking at the bait shop anyway. Morning coffee two, three times a week. Or not at all. Anyway, I won't speak of the panther. But if there is one in these woods, it changes things some. Do you have a handgun?"

The widow laughed out loud.

"Do you and I suddenly live in deepest, darkest Africa? I will not strap on a gun to walk on my land. More importantly, I will not be afraid of that cat. Just because it is here does not mean it wants to attack me."

"And if it does?" the veteran asked. She didn't answer.

"Even the *sound* of a gunshot could make it change its mind," he added.

The widow's face relaxed. "I appreciate your concern.

And your advice." She looked at her dog. "We will be careful."

"I don't mean to tend to your business," he said. "Also, I hope you'll forgive my intrusion onto your land. Might be I'm your biggest violator. I come out here pretty often. I don't know if I can just stop."

The widow's eyebrows went up and she crossed her arms.

"I go back quite a ways with that tree," the veteran said. "Before you even cared who besides you sat in its branches." He saw her eyes go hard. "Well, good day to you, ma'am. Sorry to disturb you." He turned to go.

The widow unfolded her arms. "Wait," she said. "The sign isn't for you. Thank you for checking on things. I... well...Sometimes it seems what I love here at the tree is being taken away from me." She looked at the ground. "My daddy used to say Jesus had no right to upset those tables, that folks were just trying to get by. But I know how he felt, why he was so angry."

The veteran still faced away, the fishing rod over his shoulder. He looked back at her. "Yes, ma'am." He hesitated. "You sure I can't escort you home?"

"I'm sure," she said, laughing. The veteran was not sure what she found funny. "But you may come running if you hear me scream." The dog sat down and the widow patted its head. The veteran took them both in for a moment, nodded his head and walked away. Though he wanted to, he did not look back at her.

THE VETERAN HAD BEEN ON A NORTHBOUND TRAIN 135 kilometers out of Cadiz, Spain, when his father died. A week passed before he got word.

When he caught the southbound, he took a window seat and slung his duffle bag on the floor and put his feet on it, resting his forehead against the frosted glass, feeling all over the buzz of the steel wheels on the rails.

By the time he got home, the old man was in the ground.

His house had been cleaned out. Everybody got what they wanted. Figuring him good for a few more years traveling light, that he'd serve a few more years in the homeless hippie brigade like so many returning Viet Nam vets, the heirs and assigns had left him out when they divvied up his father's stuff.

The veteran's hollow footfalls down the hall toward the back bedroom echoed like the clocking of time toward his own mortgaged future. The last time he'd seen him, the old man called him to come over, and was sitting on his bed fumbling to untie the frazzled shoelaces in his Target-brand sneakers when the veteran arrived. His father had been drinking. So the veteran spent a good deal of time looking at the sneakers that night, not wanting to get into it with the old man's eyes. They could look a hole in you.

"So you spend four damn years in the Navy getting your ticket punched to be a hobo? I told you a sailor's life is about as useful as tits on a boar hog. You could've joined the Army like I told you. Made a career of it. Be a better job than the one you ain't got now. Somebody twenty-five years old who won't work? What's that?"

The veteran nodded slow, noticing the glue was breaking loose on the toe of his father's left sneaker. The old man gave a soft, sighing groan as he bent over tugging off the shoe. He muttered something about girlie shoes and the veteran looked at the sandals on his feet, at the inner tube top straps, at the soles poking out past his toes, the discarded tire tread fashioned by hand into footwear at the site of the Cu Chi tunnel complex, forty kilometers northwest of Ho Chi Minh City. Would his father want a pair if he knew southern guerrilla forces on our side wore such sandals? Footwear didn't help much, though, in a war that took close to sixty thousand of us, and six million of them.

And then he looked at his father's thin hair falling forward, watched until his reddened face tilted back and his eyes rose like a gray dawn. There was no frown, only a malignant vacancy, and the veteran found in them a whirring and clicking forty-year rewind to nights when an open book must have smacked of girlie ways.

How many repetitions of the mantra?

There's things right outside the window that you'll never know about because you hide inside with your ass in a chair and a book in your hands. You think I'd of lived through the war if I didn't know the natural order?

He would not say: "But, Daddy, I lived. Sixty thousand boys didn't come home and here I am. Is that the natural order? Is it natural to march off to war with boots already full of blood?"

He would not say back then: "But, Daddy, I stepped over the bow of my skiff at sunset, maybe three hours ago. I stumbled home, slogging in the black mud under the weight of a stringer of fish slung over my shoulder. I scaled and gutted 'em, Daddy. I sliced fillets from the long side-meat of a dozen speckled trout. I salted the strips like I saw you do it. I wrapped them in waxed butcher paper and laid them on the refrigerator shelf while Mama was still at the grocery store. I did that, Daddy, before I sat down and balanced a book on my knee."

But he had not said those things to his father.

Why count up for him the summer days when school was out that he had worked all the hours he could get at the fishing dock on the river when the big boats came in, off-loading the catch, cleaning the decks of the trawlers. The captains folding some singles and tucking the bills into his jeans back pocket as they walked past him, his arms muscling a basket of snapper, or a coil of line, the captains bound for home or the whiskey bar out on the highway. All but a few of the dollars stacked and bound with a rubber band in an Army surplus ammunition box in the bottom of an old steamer trunk stationed at the foot of his bed, a fixture there since he could remember.

Taking his father to task would have been like diddling a short fishing pole in a July wasp nest. So easily provoked to wrath, to swarm, anger twisting into the quiet air. Then, as now, his father's eyes dared him. The old man crooked one foot over a knee and rubbed his ankle, bent forward and twisted his big toe. His left eye twitched as though he'd struck a painful nerve.

Then he straightened and placed his hands on either side of his legs, resting them on the chenille spread. "I don't understand you, boy," he said. "Don't reckon I ever did."

The veteran made no reply.

He had walked out.

Hit the road almost a year ago to the day when the news had come.

"It's a good boy to come back from way over yonder to pay last respects to your daddy," his aunt had said. Last night over fried chicken and mashed potatoes the two old aunts agreed he had his father's eyes. A first cousin at the table said, "Your daddy was much of a man, the best with a spin casting rod I ever saw. Yessir, much of a man. Mean, too, when he needed to be." And then, "I reckon that leaves you the meanest sonoafabitch in the valley."

But the veteran had not looked up from his coffee.

When he stood at the door to go, one of the aunts had given him the key to his father's apartment, the same one he'd had since coming back to Baldwin County, told him the only thing left there was the bed he died in, and she wasn't going to touch it.

"You know, I never could figure how come your mama never forgive him to come back to her. 'Specially after my brother died," she said. "He oughten to of run your daddy off like that. Folks talked for ten years. I've held my own brother the cause of your mama and daddy dyin' alone. It's a downright shame."

He could have told her we all die alone, even if our time comes in the middle of a Christmas party. She told him the probate lawyer had a letter for him. "Your daddy left you some money, son."

The veteran had left the fried chicken place alone, and now he opened the door into his father's bedroom. The blinds were closed and the curtains drawn. He flicked on the light. The room was stripped bare of the dresser and lamp and nightstand and pictures on the wall, but was yet full to ringing with memories of cautious approaches to the old man.

Come in here, boy.

There was the narrow, iron-framed bed, with a pillow,

made up as if he might be back in a minute. The closet door stood wide open. Five or six bare wire hangers hung spaced out on the rod in there.

Then he saw them. The sneakers at right angles, toe-to-toe, one turned on its side, just underneath the edge of the bed. In the layering of dust and fuzz, the shoes looked soft, lived in. Besides the bed, they were the only things left in the house. The old man always said Hell's a stylish shoe. "Heels jacked up and toes squeezed in. Gotta be true. The devil's own invention."

"Now you are dead," the veteran said, his words spreading through the silent rooms. "Cloud-tripping, barefoot, pissed off and drinking sour mash whiskey from some diamond crystal cup."

He looked around the dingy walls at the discolored rectangles where pictures had hung. I guess your heirs and assigns are funny about secondhand shoes, he'd thought. Their powdered toes refuse.

The veteran looked at the shoes. "I don't even know what size you wore," he said to the room. Then he kicked off his rubber sandals and sat cross-legged on the floor. His bare feet caterpillared into his father's sneakers, a perfect fit. He stood up, looked at the worn out shoes on his feet.

"Keep your money. I'll take the shoes."

The prodigal son had claimed another prize.

The veteran left his sandals in exchange. His aunts

would find them and they would say to someone, "See. What'd we tell you about him?"

And they would be right.

THE DEPUTY DROVE A 1979 SCOUT, SOMETHING OF A classic 4x4, powered by its original hardwinding 345 cubic inch V-8. To anyone who demonstrated an interest in such automotive details—and there were some, though never had a woman seemed to care a whit—he was pleased to tell of its particulars.

He would speak of its Dana 44 front and rear axles, Dana 20 transfer case, its A727 automatic transmission. The deputy would allow that when he got the Scout it had the typical rust, but his restoration work left the bodywork in great condition with shiny GM pearl white paint. The deputy had re-upholstered the original equipment bucket seats and rear bench seat in tan marine-grade vinyl, as well as the door panels, dash pad, and visors. This wore well in the occasional rain soaking. The Scout had jacked-up suspension and 16-inch alloy wheels and fat 33-inch Goodyear tires. Virtually every mechanical part had been renewed, at one time or another since he bought the Scout while covering the Everglades beat for the *Tribune*. During which time he had written about a black panther sighting but did not want to antagonize the game warden, choosing to let that battle go by.

The deputy loved his Scout.

Almost as much, he loved to talk about his Scout. But, with all his willingness to tell its story, he had still not revealed the total of his huge financial investment in the vehicle. He calculated that someone, in due course, would say to him, "What? All that money and the thing still doesn't have a top on it?"

At which point he would probably become defensive and say something silly like a bikini top like his was all any real off-roader needed. Silly because he never took the Scout off the road. And silly because rain fell colder in coastal Alabama than in south Florida. The deputy had decided lately that a hardtop would be useful optional equipment.

The deputy eased off the accelerator and braked as he steered around trees past where the asphalt came to a dead end. He became even less comfortable with the errand his boss had sent him on. Not to tell the widow a cockamamie tale of inbred cousins. That was for off-time. No, this was some stealth real estate mission on the company clock.

"Go back in there to see that fellow lives down at the end of River Road," the Game Warden had said. "Just ask him does he want to sell his place."

"You mean, pretend I'm interested in buying the place?"

The deputy had asked this morning in his office, frowning over his coffee cup.

"I didn't say that. You ask him if he's ever thought about selling. If he says no, tell him thanks and drive away. If he says yes, tell him you know somebody might be interested and ask him how much. I'll take care of the follow-up."

"What's the man's name?"

"I don't know. People call him Veteran. He was in 'Nam in the Navy. I think a hospital corpsman tending the wounded. I don't know."

"You want me to go unannounced to see a shell-shocked hermit?"

"Blow your horn all the way in. I don't care. And it's not a social call. You ask him a question. You leave."

"And why should I do this?"

"Because I'm the game warden and you're my deputy. Plus, you told me yourself you don't want to go back to a writer's desk."

"Okay, but, you've got a great spot on the river already. Am I allowed to ask why you're interested in this place?"

"I want two great spots on the river."

The deputy and the game warden exchanged a long look. "Sure thing, boss. I'm on it."

The surroundings were like a park, but without the benefit of a marked way. His right front wheel found a deep stump hole, fell in and jumped out, jarring his teeth. The steering wheel spun from his hand, and he cursed his slack attention and immediately gripped the wheel with his left hand.

The paper bag with a ham sandwich and chips bounced from the seat and onto the floor. The deputy had thought he might stop in a sunny spot and have his lunch. He was glad he had not opened the Gatorade he'd bought at Miss Loo's. It was still secure in the ABS cup holder he'd mounted to the transmission tunnel.

If the deputy wondered just where back in these woods he'd find this veteran fellow, he had no more to think about for the man stood directly in his path, one hand on his hip, the other holding a rifle barrel, the butt of the stock planted beside his boot. The deputy cursed again, slamming on his brakes. "I could have hit you!" the deputy yelled out the open window of the Scout.

"I could shoot you," the veteran answered. "And I might if you don't turn that wreck around and drive it off my place."

"Hey, pal, the war's over," the deputy said, killing his engine and opening the door.

"No, it's not," the veteran said, and shouldered his rifle.

"Can't you see I'm a deputy?"

"And I've got the gun."

"I do see it. Yep. And, we won't belabor the point. I just came to ask about your place here, and do you want to sell it?"

"Is there a for sale sign up that way you came from?"

"No, sir. There's not."

"There's your answer. And if you'll think a minute, it

might occur to you I didn't put a road back in here, nor even mark a trail for such a thing as you're driving."

"It's a Scout. '79 International Harvester…"

The veteran held up his hand as if to fend off more information. The deputy got his drift and dropped it.

The veteran wanted to know, "Has it got a reverse?"

"Well, yes, sir, it does," the deputy said.

"About now is when I'd be pleased for you to demonstrate it to me." The veteran poked at the air with the rifle barrel, indicating the direction back to River Road. "All clear aft," the veteran said.

"Aye, aye, Skipper," the deputy said, easing back into the cab of the Scout. Using only his side mirrors, the deputy skillfully backed out of the woods. When he glanced beyond the hood toward where the man had stood, there was no one in sight.

The deputy kept backing, weaving between sycamores and pines, carefully dodging scrub oaks and huckleberry bushes, bouncing over sinkholes and fire ant mounds. When his tires were securely on the pavement at the tail of River Road, he stopped, shut off the ignition, and retrieved his lunch from the floor. He took out the sandwich and chips, unscrewed the lid on his drink, and ate in silence.

So what're you saying to me?" The game warden pulled a pump shotgun, a Remington .870, from the glass front case in his office.

"I'm saying the man does not want to sell his land. I'm saying he left no room for misunderstanding."

"How's that?"

"He had a rifle. He's a war veteran. He doesn't screw around."

"Take this," he said to the deputy, and handed over the spotless shotgun and a box of single-aught shells. The game warden put his hand back up to the row of rifles, grazed his fingertips along their stocks, and selected a .243 Browning bolt-action rifle with a scope and sling. It had an adjustable leather strap, so the gun could be ready at hand but out of the way while looking at a map.

He gripped the rifle at the balance point on the stock, but didn't remove it from the case. With his hand on the weapon, he twisted his shoulders to face the deputy.

"This gun I've got my hand on is mighty sweet. I can grab a handful of sling with my left hand and jack it against my shoulder and drop anything that moves 250 yards away. Hundred percent of the time."

"You're not intimating you'd have a shootout with this guy because he won't sell you his land?"

"*Intimating*?"

"Whatever."

"I told you," the game warden said, "that I'm an expert with this weapon. Period. On the other hand, I'm saying pretty clear that it's not a good idea for a man to greet an officer of the law with a weapon at the ready. Period."

"I was on private property."

"Were you in uniform?"

"Yes."

"Have your badge on?"

"Yes."

"End of story," the game warden said. "For now."

"For now? That's not an end to a story. I don't know the big deal here. The man's got himself a nice place and wants to hang on to it." The deputy shook his head.

"It can be the end of the story if the vet doesn't act a fool."

The game warden pulled the Browning from the case, handled it carefully, closed and relocked the gun cabinet door. "Now let's go see about this bobcat causing a wreck out on Pensacola Highway," he said.

"I heard it when it came over the radio."

"Yeah. State troopers are dealing with the crash," the game warden said. "Two dead horses and a damn big Chevy Suburban on its roof."

The deputy asked, "And a bobcat jumps into a horse pen, spooks a pair of horses that jumps the fence and plunges into the path of an SUV?"

"That's close," the game warden said. "Pink Drummond claimed he saw the intruding cat, said it was a panther. No such a damn thing, of course. Worst part is Old Bill Fortner coming home from work plows into a couple of horses." The game warden checked his watch.

"You think it's another black bobcat? Like the one you told me about in Florida?"

"No, I do not. I think Loo and her reward posters are working some voodoo on the locals. Pretty soon Black Labs'll be dodging bullets all over the county."

"Or somebody will get a picture of a big black cat."

"Good Lord, son. I know you're bored here in Alabama, but don't go wishing up a phantom panther to bring meaning back to your life."

"Maybe I'll get the picture. Win the prize."

"Only shot you need to be taking is the one you'll squeeze off if you see a bobcat tonight. Little after five and mostly dark out there. The cat's just clocking in for work. Nothing at all unusual, I hate to break the news to you."

"Well," the deputy said, "except a bobcat mixing it up with horses. Not ordinary prey for the critter."

"You ever hear of rabies? We gotta think about rabies. You ready to do a little hunting?"

"I was actually thinking about a beer and a little football on TV," the deputy said.

"No such luck. Sorry. Grab that spotlight off the shelf. Let's take that assault vehicle of yours. You mind?"

"No, sir," he said. "Happy to oblige." The deputy stifled a grin. He loved to press his Scout into service like this. He told the game warden, "I used to love to head to the 'Glades on a renegade alligator call-in."

"Renegade 'cat is better any day," the game warden said.

The two men, each carrying a gun, walked out to the Scout and crawled into the front seat. In twenty minutes they were on the wreck scene. A big mess. Blue lights flashing. Dead horse, cut up badly, still on the highway. Another dead horse at the side of the road. Vehicle upside down in a ditch beyond the shoulder of the road, but remarkably free of body damage.

"Stop here," the game warden said, and jumped out. He turned to the deputy. "Why don't you put a top on this thing? Damn cold ride," he said. "Urban cowboy crap is what it is." And the game warden walked over to speak to the troopers while the deputy waited behind the wheel, the engine loping at idle, the heater pumping warm air around his feet. In a moment the game warden was back, crawling into the passenger's seat, saying, "Let's go west. I've got an idea."

A couple of miles and they were approaching the first of

the backwaters off Weeks Bay. The game warden told him to slow down and take the next left.

"It'll be hard to spot," he said. "Just a trail."

"What's your idea?" the deputy asked.

"That our perpetrator was out of his territory visiting that horse pen, that this is his turf and he'll be right back here, if not already, any time now. We're going to wait for him."

"In my Scout?"

"Hell, no. You're going to park this bucket. You'll handle the shotgun and I've got the rifle. We'll go on foot up and down the length of this road here three, four times. If we see a wildcat with a stump tail, we shoot it."

"Why shoot it?"

"Because it's acting damn weird. It might be rabies. We see it, it gets killed irregardless."

"Irrespective."

"What?"

"No such word," the deputy said, "as irregardless."

"The hell you say?"

"No. Look it up," the deputy said.

"I'm not talking about the damn word. I'm talking about you correcting my English. No wonder you got canned at that newspaper. It's called insubordination. There's a word you ought to look up."

"I didn't get canned at the newspaper. I quit."

"Over what?"

The deputy pulled onto a wide clearing alongside the

shoulder of the road. He looked over at the game warden, still grinning at him.

"Look. I'm not at the newspaper for lots of reasons. But the easiest one to cite is my editor's daughter. Her daddy went to the same movie we went to and he behaved like a jerk. And that's the end of that story." The deputy stepped down from behind the wheel. "Now we need to be quiet," the deputy said. "This hunting wild animals is supposed to be about stealth, I hear." He shouldered the Remington and started off down the road, the game warden beside him.

"Right," the game warden said.

"Just one other thing," the deputy said,

"Now what the hell?"

"Why're you so opposed to the idea of a black panther? I like the possibility, personally."

"You would. We already talked about that," the game warden said.

"No. I'm just saying that something wild and real like a panther would be a refreshing change from all the homogenized sprawl spreading like kudzu over the South."

"It would be refreshing if you'd stop yammering like a columnist for Mother Earth News."

"Do they still print that?" the deputy asked, stopping.

"I don't know, and I don't even care. You get my point. Now march in silence, son."

And the game warden and the deputy walked from one end of the trail near the highway, to its other end in a stand of cattails near the backwaters of Weeks Bay. They did this quietly, with stealth even. And heard not so much as a rustling of the tall grass near them.

Which did not mean there was not a cat there, somewhere, watching.

THE WIDOW KNEW IT WAS LATE, MAYBE PAST MIDNIGHT. She stopped, still. Above the sweep of the wind she heard the yowl of a cat. Or, thought she heard it. Had she been sober, she might have crept more carefully through the brush.

She did not often soak her episodes of sadness in red wine. Four, maybe five times since her husband's death. But the bottle of Shiraz had seemed a good companion for her little bit of melancholia. She had not eaten since before noon, and the first glass made her face tingle and warmed her chest. By the third glass, she was drunk.

When the bottle was empty, she had struck out for Ghosthead Oak, stopping in her yard at the dim edge of yellow light from her porch light to consider her .410 shotgun. Hell no, she'd thought, this is my place, this is land that I walk in silence. I am not on safari.

Quick as a mullet's jump, the waning moon's light was blocked, and the widow looked up to see a fast-flying fist of cloud. She once again sought the path ahead of her, making her way in deep shade almost as if she'd ducked into a cave. Though she couldn't see well in this dark, she knew from her place on the path that she was close to the tree. Even as a young girl she'd believed she could walk to the tree wearing a blindfold. This rising of the ground, the soil growing firmer underfoot meant she was within a hundred yards.

Beyond Ghosthead Oak, at the edge of the deep woods, the ground rose. In the other direction it sloped slightly downward and became soft underfoot and bristled again with sea grass and sparse scrub brush. The widow had heard her father say it was an oddity, this island of hard high ground in the Weeks Bay lowland, as if it answered some cosmic plea to support one tree.

By now in the widow's going, the air had gone pitch black. She thought she heard the cat again, this time from where she had just come, and jerking her head to look behind, the widow stumbled and fell. She rolled and was up on her feet again, though the wine in her head made her unsteady until she drew a breath or two. She extended her hand, as if that would provide balance, and walked on more slowly. Her eyes could make out nothing. Then the sound of the wind grew muffled, and she knew she had arrived underneath the canopy of Ghosthead Oak. She stopped still. She listened and heard nothing.

Then the clouds parted and a sagging moonlit branch looked as thick as an entire tree's trunk and reminded her as it had since she was a toddler of the neck of a grazing brontosaurus.

She wished for her dog and wondered would it follow clawless tracks in the mud of the sloughs and wetlands? Would it go creeping through the low country looking for a cat black as a raven along the slippery banks of the canals and creeks that ebbed and flowed with the tide's wet heave-ho of lunar will? Did her dog mean to defend its territorial claims?

The widow had heard the news of a wildcat panicking a pair of horses so that they were driven white-eyed onto the highway and into the path of an oncoming Chevy Suburban that flipped and skidded fifty-seven feet on its roof, leaving the mare dead and the stud busted up for the vet to put down.

The widow imagined how she would have asked her husband what he believed was driving this cat's unusual and erratic behavior and he would have told her some reason without waffling, correct or not. So would her father have been quick with an answer. Both would have paused, however, at the news of a panther in the county.

A marauding bobcat had once paid a predawn visit to the crawlspace underneath her father's house and the raucous wakeup call had startled her from her sleep. She'd hardly got her feet on the floor when she flinched at the ear-ringing report from her father's twelve-gauge. The explosion came from a few yards back of the house. In half a minute her father had stumbled into the kitchen rubbing sleep from his eyes, his hair every which way. I missed him, was all he said as he wobbled past her, stood the shotgun in the corner and went back to bed.

She thought she heard another brief snarl. The veteran had been right. The noise of the report from a shotgun would be enough to chase away a curious cat, and she wished now she had brought the gun her father gave her.

The effects of the wine numbed the widow's head, and she thought she heard someone coming. She listened again. She heard nothing, only the wind pushing across the low country. Live oaks kept their leaves year-round, and the flutter of green in the wind recalled coastal summer days even in bleak December, and on this winter's night the heavy green had a silver patina. The spread of foliage on Ghosthead Oak was thick, allowing moonlight to spatter the ground only here and there near the trunk. She could see nothing.

Again, she heard a muffled sound like a cough.

And for another moment heard nothing. But then she heard two voices trading hushed talk, drawing nearer to Ghosthead Oak.

She moved quickly outside the perimeter of the canopy, several yards into the tall grass, and dropped to her knees. She pulled in a long slow breath of cold night air, hoping it would erase some of the effects of the wine. The moon broke free of the racing cloud cover and lit the weeds around her, but darkness held its own underneath the tree. The widow could not see who it was going there, though she knew from the direction of their voices that the two were now at the base of the tree.

"Shhhh," said one of them. "We have to keep it down. The old woman who owns this land will shoot our eyes out. And I'm not kidding about that."

"Oh, you're lying, Link," said the other, in a normal speaking voice. "I don't believe that for a minute. You ever look at her? How pretty she still is? Woman like that wouldn't hoist a gun against a gypsy thief. Not even if he were toting off everything she owned."

"Well, by God, what about that veteran dude? Tell me you don't think some hairy-backed war nut would draw a bead on your skinny butt. He's holed up in a trailer just down yonder. Now shut up while I dig."

"You mean if the sorry fool hid the stuff here like he was s'posed to."

"Oh, it'll be here. I put his ten-dollar bill in the fruit jar like last time."

The widow was trying to place who the two boys were. They sounded young. She thought she remembered the name Link, but their voices weren't familiar. The widow's knees were getting wet on the soft, damp ground, and she sat back on her calves.

These boys, she thought, had come up with a clever way for buying their "stuff." Probably marijuana. They could wait outside any package store and soon enough get someone to buy whiskey. This transaction, she surmised, was almost as easy. Leave money in a buried jar for the dealer. Come back next night and dig up the jar and retrieve the goods. As drunk as she was, she felt an urge to just yell at them to get off her land. But, it was too unpredictable, she knew, and could go all wrong. She decided to let this little drama unfold without doing something to make the story turn out worse.

Though they had stopped talking, the widow could hear the two boys huffing and digging, with their hands she guessed. She turned her head, tilted her ear, hoping to catch whatever else they might say. On some level, the widow was glad for the distraction from her heavy mood. She shifted her weight, was about to get back up on her knees for a moment when there arose into the night such a fierce, prolonged loud wail that her flesh tingled with goose bumps. She had to stifle a yelp.

It was the cat, and it was close. The screech had come from the direction of the boys. The way to Ghosthead Oak from the road, a path the widow never took, was now blocked for the boys. A big cat challenged them for passage there.

The whistle of the wind in the night air was louder, constant, but muffled and dampened as if heard from inside a house. The two boys' labor had ceased and they let up their own cry. The panther had startled them good. The widow could hear them cursing and struggling to get up and get going, awkwardly trying to find their bearings.

"I told you we shoulda brought a gun," said the one called Link. "I told you."

That was the last thing the widow heard them say. The two boys were on the run.

By the time they made their noisy exit, the widow knew that the trunk of the tree was where she wanted it to be. She would put her back to it and have only her front side to guard. She would kick the teeth out of any creature that came within a leg's reach. The way she had dealt with the Boxer dog, which she had kicked in its side near the back steps of her cottage. She'd gone out for a few sticks of firewood, had the sawn and split pecan logs in her arms when the dog, a neighbor's pet, took a stance in front of her and refused to let her go back inside. When it came close, without dropping the firewood, she landed her foot full force in the dog's side and it gave a big *oomph* and ran away crying.

The widow could not judge the determination of this cat, but surmised it would be more set in its purpose, whatever that might be. Still, adrenaline poured into her blood, and she knew she would stand her ground and fight, if it came to that.

She brushed the mud from her knees and loped and stumbled through the bushes, blinking at weeds whipping her face. It seemed to be taking way too long to reach the tree trunk, and she wondered in the darkness if she'd somehow taken off in the wrong direction. Suddenly her worry was answered by a head-on jarring collision with Ghosthead Oak. She staggered back and stood at last arm's length in front of the mountainous tree trunk.

The widow immediately turned her back to the tree and pressed herself against its roughly furrowed hide. She could hear, but growing fainter, the babble of the running boys. She was alone again, and neither phrase nor word passed before her mind. She was completely grounded in the moment and only saw the dappling of the moonlight on the leafy ground, only smelled the little nuances of mud and grass and fish and water tossed about on the light wind, only heard the sweep of that breeze high up in the branches of Ghosthead Oak, only felt the grooved hide of the tree against her back and the thumping of her heart.

She could see a moving shape to her right. She pressed her back harder into the bark of the tree. The breadth of the uneven trunk was so great that its curve could not be detected. She wanted to turn her face and put her cheek to the rough bark. And she might have done that but for the closeness of the low and hoarse hissing from the cat as it drew slowly nearer.

She couldn't help but wonder would this encounter be less fearsome if it were not in the dead of a moonshadow night. She remembered what she'd said to her husband just seconds before he died, that she was glad for the daylight. But it was dark and every one of the widow's senses was keen for confrontation, her muscles and her bones welded to the purpose at hand.

Then, like a sudden rocky hazard appearing to a sailor from out of the fog, the cat's face materialized in a circle of bright moon light within ten feet, and it was a visage of curved yellow teeth and bloody green eyes. She yielded to reflex and kicked out with her right leg and almost fell. The cat did not blink, only lowered its head and advanced slowly. The widow knew this panther would not be chased away like a house cat. What she did not know was what would come next. She suddenly wished for her husband's hands on her arm. Her notion of fighting the good fight in this instant seemed utterly preposterous.

In a lightning fast flurry of legs and tail and black fur, with bared fangs and a deep voice, a dog blew past the widow's knees and banged into the cat, and the dog and the cat rolled into a ball of writhing legs and paws and teeth. Black and black. Even in the dark, she recognized her dog. Her own protective instincts exploded inside her, and when she believed she had a clear shot at the cat's rear end she gave a sidelong kick at the mess of snapping jaws and churning legs tumbling on the ground. The cat's thick tail looked itself like a thing alive, whipping and flexing. The widow aimed, as best she could, with the broad side of her foot and heel, knowing her bare toes would be more vulnerable. She screamed as the blow landed solidly, squarely on the cat's hindquarters, and it spun the beast around.

It also gave her dog the tiniest advantage, and, in a blood scrape like this, it would not be wasted. The dog bit into the cat's neck, just ahead of its left shoulder, and the inch-long teeth top and bottom of the black dog's jaws sank into panther flesh. Flinging its head side to side, the dog had the cat in a death grip and she loved each of its one hundred and twenty pounds, grateful it was not a lap dog. Suddenly the cat twisted and somehow found purchase against the dog's chest with its forepaws, raked its razor claws downward, and, in an instant, was loose. The dog yipped, and the cat leaped back, and in a breath was gone from sight. Her dog was on its side in the leaves.

She was crying when she fell to her knees and put her face against the dog's side, sure that he was down and badly hurt, though she had not the time to discern its injuries. She spoke the dog's name and it was hardly out of her mouth when it rolled and stood on wobbly legs and licked her on the face. The widow wept and laughed and fell on the ground and the dog's big wet tongue, warm and rough, pulled across her cheek and the corner of her eye.

She put her hand to the cuts on the dog's chest, felt warm blood, and pushed the wetness with her fingers and felt only surface wounds.

"Okay, okay, girl. We made it."

The widow crawled toward the tree, got herself up to sitting and leaned her back against the tree. The big dog put its wet black head on her lap. The two of them waited for their breathing to settle. The moon slid behind a cloud and the canopy of the oak tree held the darkness close around them and the rise and fall of their chests became slow and rhythmic and they were soon both sleeping.

HE HEARD THE COMMOTION AND ROLLED OVER QUIETLY
and sat on the edge of his bed. It was black enough inside
the Airstream that when he closed his eyes he detected no
difference in the darkness. He kept them closed.

He extended his foot and found his pants on the floor,
dragged them over and tugged them up to his knees. He
stood and buckled his pants and walked into the galley area.
In the darkness he found his cigarettes and lighter on the
table beside the paperback.

The veteran flicked open his Zippo. He squinted when
the tiny wheel tossed a spark and spun light into the trailer.
He lit the Camel, took an easy draw and left the cigarette
hanging in his mouth while he opened the screen door into
the pitch of night and found his boots on the stoop. He pulled
them on, reached back and got his big coat off the hook.
With that and no shirt, he set out in the direction of the big
tree. That's where the racket had come from. Sounded like a
death fight and at least one of the creatures was a dog.

It had been years since he'd owned the mutt he called Ballard, a shepherd-hound mix that would bite the hand feeding it. The veteran and the dog had got along, partners until the dog died of cancer, its face in his lap. Just sighed and quit breathing.

He'd buried Ballard under the front of the Airstream, in the shade where the dog liked to lay on hot days. The veteran had no thought of getting another, but he had a rapport with the creatures that drew even the bad ones to his side for a pat on the head. He would know in twenty minutes if the dog out there had a gash in its neck or belly.

The going was easy and familiar. He had some history around the place, and if it counted for nothing else, it kept him from falling down on a night's walk. Sometimes he thought about the widow just down the river, a woman alone. His age. Though he only saw her now and again in her old station wagon, she'd been pleasant enough when he saw her the other day. Maybe she'd like to share some of his homemade gumbo, probably the best on the river. He wanted company now and then. They had Ghosthead Oak in common. It belonged to her, but it was his, too.

Even before she granted him green card status.

Plus, she was pretty.

The veteran's eyes grew accustomed to the night and he could make out the landscape well in the dark. The wind was abating and the clouds flew farther east. Beyond the moon's silver wash, the sky was dirty with stars. He directed his attention back to the path, and, in sight of the tree, he slowed.

Listened.

Nothing.

He stepped carefully, curious what he'd find. Considered he might have brought a towel, or a pillowcase. Something for a make-do bandage, just in case.

But nothing brought along could have prepared him for what he found.

There was a dog alright, looking at him from where it lay beside the outstretched legs of a woman who leaned back against the tree.

"What the hell?" the veteran asked. He looked behind him and to either side. Not a sound. Not a movement. The dog didn't move, though its expression was tight and wary, certainly following his motion. *Damn.* He wanted a cigarette, but wouldn't dare light up. Fact of the business, what to do now? The veteran ran down the short list of options: Check on the woman and dog. Go back to bed.

He squatted and made a slight kissing sound to see if the dog was on his side. The dog got up and came to him, its tail wagging, and sniffed the veteran's outstretched hand. Right away, he knew this dog had been in the fight. There was matted blood on its side and neck and chest. Nothing serious.

"You must have won, pal," he said. "What about your lady friend? Should we check it out?"

The black dog turned and took a few steps toward its mistress, stopped and looked back at the veteran. Okay, he said to himself, wondering, was she packing? He'd made the suggestion to her himself. He was shot at in Viet Nam, but that was for pay.

He didn't have to get closer than just outside arm's reach to discover the woman was drunk. He could smell the wine. From what he could tell in the low light, she had no marks on her, no cuts or scrapes. He watched her breathing to see that it was regular. She was passed out, but she seemed okay and she was on her own property.

"Okay, pup," he told the black dog, "You seem to have it all under control, so I'm turning this back over to you. The cat comes back, try bluffing your way through it this time. Growl. Give it a rest for this night." He patted the dog. It seemed to understand and lay down beside the woman, parking its muzzle on her thigh. She didn't move.

The wind was still but the night air was chilly, and it crossed his mind to fetch a blanket for her lap and shoulders. He didn't know how long she'd be passed out. Her heavy jacket might not keep her warm enough. On the other hand, if she did get cold, maybe she'd wake up and go home.

"Oh, hell," he said aloud. "Enough back and forth. Okay, pup, your lady is drunk. I gotta trust you to keep the situation under control for a minute. I'll be back."

Back at his trailer, the veteran took a folded heavy woolen blanket from a cupboard above his bed. He stuffed it underneath his arm, took two steps to the kitchen area and reached into the narrow broom closet for his Winchester. With the blanket held close, the rifle in his hand, he went back out the door. Going at a good clip, he was soon back at Ghosthead Oak. The dog and the widow just like he left them, her eyes still closed and now and then a short repetition of soft snoring. The dog hardly lifted its head as he cautiously drew close to them.

He draped the blanket over the sleeping woman with the dog's approval. It pushed itself back some and curled more tightly against the widow. He patted the dog's head and slipped away, walking backward, into the bushes on the perimeter. The veteran sat on the ground, the rifle on his knees, his eyes on the widow.

THE DEPUTY PARKED HIS SCOUT UNDERNEATH A LIVE oak, a smaller sibling of the big tree the game warden had taken him to see. The branches of this smaller tree in the widow's yard were draped with Spanish moss, a grayish white Bromeliad-beard that clumped and hung down two feet or more, waving in the breeze. So thick was the tree's moss that it looked as if it were dressed in a burial shroud. The deputy guessed the effect at twilight would be eerie.

The big tree's heavy branches, he recalled, were not festooned with this Spanish moss, only thin flags of it here and there like horses' tails dangling, caught on the gray bark. The whole scene here—the tiny tin-roofed cottage and its faded white clapboards and peeling mildewy green shutters, its broad veranda across the front—seemed to have been inspired by the canvas of some Louisiana folk artist. Lifted, perhaps, from an oil study of the bald cypress swamps and murky bayous of Atchafalaya Basin and some simple raised Creole cottage that teetered over a yard where dogs would crawl from beneath the house to bite you. He stepped from his Scout but held onto the door handle, waiting for a hound to attack from around the corner.

When no dog charged him, the deputy let go the car door and crossed the yard scattered here and there with scraps of fallen tufts of Spanish moss and a bumper crop of acorns. Otherwise, the ground was bare, a soil and sand mix the color of weathered khaki. Bleached white shells from the driveway were strewn about the yard, and three big red clay pots going green with algae were each overgrown with Sago palms threatening to topple in the next strong wind. Or, the deputy thought, more likely they'd forever lean unbalanced. He climbed the steps to the porch and crossed its broad plank floor to the front door, opened the screen and knocked. A tentative knock, really. Unlike himself. Maybe he wasn't ready to talk to the widow after all.

He looked over his shoulder toward his Scout. Wondered if from any angle or vantage point in this yard he could see the top of the big tree. It must be within a skip and a jump, as they say. He heard footfalls within the cottage and returned his attention to the unpainted door crafted with tight-grained pine boards from a very old tree.

The deputy cleared his throat.

The doorknob jiggled and turned. A cheek, then half a face appeared in the crack. Slowly the space widened and a beautiful woman confronted the deputy, maybe in her fifties. Or, was she forty? No way could she be sixty, as the game warden suggested. Her dark hair and fair skin caught the light coming in the door and appeared soft, touched with highlights. Her eyes were clear as a child's. Fashion models and actresses accomplished this look with careful rest and expert makeup and expensive lighting. This woman, the widow he had pictured like the green-tinted witch in Oz, was the most beautiful woman he had ever seen. Of any age.

He realized with a blush that he was staring, and silent as a brick. Nor did she speak, only looked at him with unblinking eyes that seemed to darken to a deeper hazel, from almost gray to green.

"Ah, ma'am…I'm a deputy. Just started working for the game warden. But, I used to be a reporter, so I was thinking about freelancing a piece for the city magazine over in Mobile," he said. "I saw the oak tree on your property, and, ah…well, I'd like to bring a photographer and do a feature story on the tree. I'd like your permission to do that."

"Please," she said, and a freshening breeze at his shoulder accentuated her pause. She said again, "Please don't write about the tree. It would only make things worse."

"I'm sorry, I don't understand," the deputy said.

"And you couldn't," she said, "unless you lived in this house. My people have lived on this land for a hundred and seventy-three years. Unless you know what roots like that mean…"

"A story about the tree wouldn't change that, ma'am."

"If you wrote about the last place to stand at twilight

to hear a train whistle, so many would come, keeping up such a clamor that no one could hear it." Something of what she'd said caught the deputy off guard. He looked away for a moment.

"My piece would be very low key," he said. "I wouldn't play it up like a tourist attraction."

"It's already that. But worse. Please, it would only bring more bottles and cans and garbage if you wrote about Ghosthead Oak. I saw my daddy on his knees in prayer one time in my life. Under that tree."

"But couldn't we share some of what's special about the tree with other people?"

"I don't want to share their profanity, hear their fights and parties until the daylight. There's even drug dealing. The tree is—well, it's just hard to make you see, but, please."

"Ma'am, I…"

"Please? My father is buried there." She looked straight into his eyes. "Your game warden said he could be relocated."

"Why? What? He wants you to move your father's body?"

"Please, you'll have to ask him."

"I'm sorry, ma'am, that's just weird, makes no…"

The deputy stopped in mid sentence. Looked away. Looked back at her. He said nothing, caught in her gaze. For some odd reason, by some loose association, he was reminded of a Japanese painting hanging in his mother's house in Tuscaloosa. A tiny *ie* set on a mountainside. How many times had its imperfect beauty, the muted gray and green washes, the touches of faded blue, arrested his mind, stopped him in that narrow hallway to wonder at the conveyance of such tender longing from a small rectangle of framed paper.

He swallowed and let his eyes look away for a moment before meeting hers full on, saying, "Of course, ma'am. I won't do the story."

The widow said, softly, "Thank you." She lowered her face and put her hand on the door to ease it closed.

"Ah, do you mind"—the deputy almost blurted out, as though he were remembering something at the last second— "if I come back to visit the tree? I could knock and let you know."

"I don't know that anyone in twenty years has asked permission," she said, holding the door only just open, the dimly lit room behind her soft as the shade from a rain cloud in summer. "You don't have to stop here. You have my permission."

"I don't mind," he said.

The widow said nothing, and closed the door.

The deputy wondered had he seen a faint smile. Had she known he would knock on her door every day for the flimsiest of reasons? Before he could follow that phantasm very far he was met with the certain presence of a big black dog standing at the corner of the house, staring at him. He almost knocked on the widow's door again. But a phrase popped into his head. Who'd uttered it? Churchill? *Do that which you fear, and watch fear disappear.*

"We'll just have to see about that," the deputy said aloud to no one.

The deputy eased off the porch, keeping his face turned to the left to watch the dog. He couldn't remember what he was supposed to do. Walk nonchalantly. Walk backward with his arms flapping. He decided to run like hell, a far more certain course of action in his experience and inclination.

He had only the briefest slice of time to consider had he instinctively locked his truck door. The deputy immediately decided the hood of the Scout was the island for this little storm. Ten feet from the vehicle, the deputy began his leap. Landed square in the middle of his hood with both feet and felt the metal buckle underneath him, then a kind of a twisting handspring onto the roof, coming down in a crouch in the direction of the attacking dog.

Which sat precisely where he had first seen it.

Until the widow opened her front door and called the dog onto the porch and inside the house. This time he was sure he saw, all the way from here to there, a smile on her face. A big smile.

THE CROW AND THE MOCKINGBIRD FLEW SIDE BY SIDE, in the direction of the giant oak, not yet in sight. The crow banked quickly, and the harassing mockingbird fell away, but only for a moment before resuming its dive-bombing attack. The crow had flown too close to a holly tree the mockingbird had claimed as its own. And, for mockingbirds, once such a stake is made, its fiercely territorial nature is brought to the fore when a challenge is assumed. Sometimes the small gray bird would assault cats and even people.

Behind the pair of scrapping birds, off to the west from within a bulge of black clouds, there came a flash of lightning more brilliant than the afternoon sun, and the air shuddered with the concussion that followed.

The crow could feel the thunder in the chambers of her hollow bones.

Rain was approaching.

And the two birds continued in their jittery formation, the crow in the lead flying low at the tree tops, darting past a house where a black dog lifted her head off her paws to watch them go. Just before the crow angled off to the southeast toward the marshy wetland that was the broad perimeter of Weeks Bay, the mockingbird gave the crow a good crashing thump, tried to sink its beak into the black feathers, and then gave up the fight.

The crow flew on toward the spot of high ground and the oak tree that was its overlord. From the topmost branches of the big live oak the crow could see the crystalline reflection of waves white-capping on Mobile Bay farther to the west, the sun's glare on the water somehow incongruous with the front's dark approach, and yet provocative and alluring.

The crow came in sight of the oak tree's jade canopy, its dome like some mountainous head crowning toward the sky. Billowing, heavy clouds ran before a wall of gray rain. The storm dragged a quick cloak of darkness over the land and the temperature fell ten degrees in four minutes. The crow flew to the branch and the very spot where she roosted, though the edge of night was still twenty-five hundred miles east and almost a three-hour wait.

The rain, however, would be here within minutes. She could see it approaching like heavy smoke enshrouding the landscape. She waited.

The first fat drop thunked the crow on the head, but she didn't budge.

Only blinked.

A few more random raindrops, coming faster, a great

sssshhhhhh filling the air with sound, a deluge upon the land. The crow hopped to a lower branch, and then another as her black feathers shed the water. She flew deeper into the green, stopped on a limb the rain had not yet reached, then dropped on spread wings to the ground, still dry, and stood there. She was alone. Surrounded only by the terrific rattle and hum of a coastal downpour *rata-tat-tat* on her big umbrella.

ER FATHER HAD GIVEN HER HAND IN MARRIAGE, AND she had asked the goat herder if he would also have the wedding ceremony at her father's house. "I want my father to know," she told him, "that he is no less important to me when I have become a wife."

"And remind him he gets me in the bargain. A lowly goat herder steals the hand of his daughter."

"Better to him by far than the highbrow lawyer you once were," she said. "And he loves the cheese you make."

"*We* make," he said.

"Okay. The cheese we make, and the honey we collect."

"What about the love we make?" he had asked her with a grin. "Does he know about that cottage industry?"

She swatted him with a willow branch she'd broken off a tree as they walked along the pathway to the big tree swinging a picnic basket—a bottle of red wine and some of their cheese and honey, a fat loaf of bread he'd baked the day before.

"Well, no more of that," she said. "Not until after the

wedding. I want that night to be special."

"And if you just so much as try to change your mind about waiting," he said, "I will be so disappointed and put out with you." She flicked him on the shoulder again with the willow branch.

"Did you know," he asked, playfully snatching the willow limb from her hand, "that willows are not common in this area?"

"Yes, that's the very reason my grandfather planted the tree."

"I wonder," he said, gazing off, "did an Aztec on pilgrimage here, a shaman or warrior god, plant Ghosthead Oak? It seems such a mystical thing to me, that tree."

Always in the company of the oak tree, the goat herder fell quiet for some spell, becoming distracted and contemplative, saying now and again, *What?* She knew at those moments he was not really listening to her when she talked to him as they reclined in the shade of the big oak. He never wanted to spread their blanket at the trunk of the tree, to lean their backs against it. He preferred, instead, to position their blanket and basket under one certain branch of such huge girth it could have been mistaken for a tree trunk itself. At its eighty-foot mark, it swung low to within five feet of the ground, curving gently back toward the sky at its leafy tip. The ground underneath was soft and cool.

She lay beside him, saying how she hoped to learn more about his church. "My mother was strict Baptist and more than once warned me about the Papists." She noticed he was not attending at all to what she said. So she clowned, telling him how she hoped to train his goats to pull a wagon, and have them take her to town once a week, how maybe she'd tear out the entire kitchen at his place. "When I'm the missus, I'll put in a barbecue pit, and we'll feast on roasted goat." He only nodded, and said, "Uh huh."

Only when she had kissed him did he pay attention.

Then he looked at her. Closely. Surprised, even. And more surprised when she made love to him there in the shade of Ghosthead Oak.

EVENING'S SHADOWS ADVANCED IN THE FARTHER WOODS. The veteran was on his knees, setting out some cast iron plants he'd found tossed into a heap on the riverbank, when the widow walked into the clearing. She was dragging a double-bitted ax by its handle, blood drying down to her lace-up hiking boots in brown rivulets below a two-inch cut on her calf. Her gray dress was dirty, bunched up, the belt at her waist holding the hem above her boots, which looked out of place paired with the long dress and baggy white sweater.

"Jesus. You okay?" The veteran jumped to his feet, looking down the path to see was there another surprise following her, maybe somebody with a worse wound.

"It's not as bad as it looks," she said. "But I need some help."

"You want to go in out of the cold?"

"Please," she said.

"Better leave that out here," he said, nodding toward the

ax. She looked to see where she might put it, but gave it to the veteran and he leaned it against the Airstream. The door was not locked, and the veteran let them inside, signaling with a nod for the widow to go first. A small heater buzzed, warming the inside of the trailer.

"Can I get you something to drink?" he offered.

She said, "Yes, I'd like that."

"Some folks," he told her, staying with small talk, "would rather drink coffee on cold days like this."

"I'm fine with iced tea anytime," she said. "I drink my coffee in the morning."

"Can I take your sweater?"

"I'll just keep it on," she answered.

He opened his palm in the direction of the dinette table, offering the woman to sit as he turned and took a jug of tea from the refrigerator. The veteran poured for her a glass of sweet tea, reached into a basket for a lemon, saying, "You want to tell me what you've been chopping?"

When she didn't answer, he took a knife from the drawer and began slicing the lemon, looked over his shoulder in her direction. She was staring down at her hands one on top of the other on the table. Then she let her eyes travel about the trailer. He thought she might be stalling. He became more curious. He put a chunk or two of ice in the glasses on the counter.

Still, she surveyed his tiny home. Okay, he thought, then himself began to wonder how a woman found such economy of space in a kitchen, the compact arrangement of cupboards, the small stove and refrigerator and sink fit into a working space of about five feet. He expected anyone would appreciate the varnished cherrywood interior curves. His books were neatly placed on homemade pineboard shelving, and centered on a side table by the couch were three hardbacks and an open paperback.

"You've got some good books. Hemingway. Faulkner."

"I read a lot as a kid. Still do."

The veteran let his eyes move over his stuff inside the trailer. He was glad he'd put away last night's whiskey bottle. A whiskey bottle on an afternoon table would suggest more than his nightly drink. But then, as he thought more about it, why the hell should he care to keep house or appearances in any kind of way for anybody else in the world? She was the one who'd shown up out of nowhere. If she found something not to her liking, the way back was the same as the way in.

Then, he caught himself getting defensive, all on his own. He smiled.

"Something funny?" she asked.

"Just something in my head. No big deal."

He poured sweet tea for them both and handed her a glass. She took it and held it, not drinking yet, waiting for him to sit down.

"I do remember you from school," she said, and then looked down at the table. "I, too, have lost count of years it seems but some memories keep their own count. They come and go according to their own will."

"Memories are alive like the life that got them here," he said. "Couldn't be any other way. Here's your tea. I brew it slow in the sun. Don't use much sugar, but it suits me."

She tasted the tea. He saw her eyes approve, and she took a long swallow. "It's very good," she said.

"Thanks."

"I'm sorry to just show up on your place."

"I don't have a phone," the veteran said. "Don't expect you could've dropped me a line under the circumstances." He looked at the crusty gash on her leg. "Stopping by would be about your only option."

"Yes," she said.

"Fellow like me's gotta wonder, though, just what drama is back in the direction you came from."

The widow sat her tea down and folded her hands in her lap. "It's about the other night," she said.

"What other night?" the veteran asked. "I would've laid money it was something to do with that chopping ax you dragged up here."

She ignored his remark. "Two nights ago," she said, "when you came to Ghosthead Oak and found my dog and me there."

"I kind of thought you were, well…asleep, you know. Once I knew you and the pup were okay, I didn't want to bother you."

"I was drunk, almost passed out. I blinked my eyes open and saw you there. I was terrified. Then my dog went to you—some guard dog she is—and then I recognized you."

"I heard a commotion like a dogfight and came to see what had happened. Thought a pooch might be hurt."

"She could have been. The panther I told you about, it came to the tree looking for trouble. I don't know how it would have gone but for my dog. She charged the panther, taking up for me. She could have been killed. I kicked the cat."

"You kicked a panther?" The veteran was skeptical.

"As hard as I could. Maybe I screamed when I did it."

"Not a bad idea, I suppose." The veteran drank some tea. "I still think the idea of a handgun is a good one." He looked away as though the answer to the cat's odd behavior—or this bizarre social call—might be found in a corner of his trailer. "Usually a creature like that wants to stay clear of people, not come after them. Though sometimes a she-cat will act up that way," he said, "if you get close to her cubs."

"This one just seemed to have its eye on me. It's a male, too. I saw it in the daylight, remember?

The veteran swirled the ice in his tea glass. "Strange," he said. "Oh, well, here's to your bravery." The veteran lifted his tea glass. The widow picked up her glass from the table, met his with a clink, and his nod with a thin smile.

"But you didn't come here to tell me about your run-in with some jungle cat, even though it's a good story."

"No. But I did want to thank you for leaving me be the other night."

"What would I have done? Banged you on the head with my caveman's club?"

"It's just that you eased so quietly away. Patted my dog on the head. I don't know. It was an act of kindness. For which I'm grateful." She drank a sip of tea. "And, I came to explain myself," she said.

"I was wondering when you were going to get around to that ax."

"Not that. I mean to say I don't often pass out in the woods at night."

"It's your tree, I reckon. Not anything you need to say to me."

"I know. Still—" The widow stopped talking abruptly, to consider for a second, then, "I wish to hire you."

"I don't hire out much," the veteran said.

"I don't know how to use an ax well enough to do what I have to do."

"I can see that."

"But you can, I'm sure. And you keep to yourself. That's important. Why I'm here can't be talked about."

"I'm listening."

"I want to hire you to girdle the big oak."

"What the hell are you talking about?"

"I would do it myself if I knew how," the widow said. "If you won't do it, I'll go to the Neptune Club and hire one of the drunks off a barstool. A hundred dollar bill, or three, or five of them. Someone will take the job."

"I don't doubt it, ma'am. But you're telling me you yourself have been out chopping on that tree?" The veteran frowned and stood up. He leaned against the counter, folded his arms and stared at her.

"Have you read Steinbeck?" Her eyes were full.

"Sure. What the hell's that got to do with what's on the table? You still drunk?"

"*Of Mice and Men.* Remember? When the cowhands in the bunkhouse decided Candy's old dog should be put down?"

"I remember."

"Candy wouldn't admit any such thing. But even Slim agreed. Then Carlton said he'd do it."

"Yeah, and…"

"And when Carlton tied that leather thong around the dog's neck and led him outside and Candy turned over on his bunk and just stared at the wall? Waiting. The men talked on, but everybody was looking at Candy, whose back was to them. And they all waited." Now tears broke free and rolled down the widow's cheek, but she did not blink or look away. "That is the saddest scene in literature. And the shot rang out and Candy still did not move. That was his dog. His best friend. And another man was putting a bullet in its head."

The veteran swallowed, uncrossed his arms. He put his hands in the pockets of his jeans.

"Candy should have put his dog down."

"I'll go along with that. I will," he said.

"I refuse to let Ghosthead Oak be taken from me and turned into a ward of the state. My father's body dug up and hauled somewhere so tourists can trample the land of my grandfathers with the next place on their minds.

"Whoa, whoa. Slow down here." The veteran sat at the table across from the widow. "Taken from you? You need to tell me what the hell you're talking about."

"You don't read the newspaper?"

"Do you see one in here?"

"No," she said without looking around. "I brought this," she said. The widow reached into her jacket pocket and produced a folded piece of newspaper. She opened it and placed it on the table. Looking down, she tapped the headline. A curling lock of hair black as a raven's wing fell forward and the widow tucked it behind her ear.

The veteran took half a minute to skim the piece.

"Sonofabitch."

"Something like that," she said.

"But can they do that? Just take your land? I thought they could only play that card when they want to put a road through somebody's front yard."

"The law says—and believe me I've read the phrase a hundred times—it says the government can 'expropriate private property for public use with payment of compensation.' Expropriate is another word for steal. You go fishing, and I'll drag off your trailer and leave a check for you nailed to the tree."

"Yeah, and you might get wounded in action."

"I did," she said. "See." And she lifted her leg and tugged up her dress.

"But, what, you chop on the tree, and a little on your leg, and that does what? Help me out here."

"The tree is old. Facing its new fate, it's had enough. My grandfather prophesied this day would come. And it's my charge to do what has to be done. I will not lie on my cot and wait for the news."

"But you'll ask me to do the dirty work?"

"I tried to do it myself and I cannot."

"What makes you think you've got the right to sit judge and jury on that tree?"

"Every farmer in this county has sold the timber off his property," she said, "at one time or another. Call it that."

"That's bullshit, and you know it. Ghosthead Oak is not timber."

"No, it isn't. And it's not another freak show giant Florida alligator." The widow folded the newspaper and put it back into her pocket. She pushed her fingers through her long hair, over her head and down her neck, twisting a handful of it over her shoulder. There was wildness in her eyes.

"Maybe you know this game warden," she said. "He's driving the whole thing."

"I know the family name. Figure they own most of this

end of the county," he said. The veteran looked behind him and picked up his pack of Camels. He asked, "You mind?"

"No," she said. "But thank you for asking."

"So, what the hell's in it for him?" the veteran asked, lighting his cigarette.

"I'm not sure," she said. She looked at the backs of her hands. The widow continued. "The game warden came to my place wanting me to sell him three acres around the tree. I wouldn't. Now, somehow it's come to this. From what he's quoted as saying, he wants everyone to think he's some Boy Scout leader. But he's up to something."

The veteran said nothing. Locked in a stare with her, he processed this piece of news, compared it to the offer from the green deputy two days ago. The widow took note of his pause.

"What?" she asked.

"Nothing," he said. He took a long draw on his cigarette, held the smoke in his chest while he flicked the ashes into an oyster shell. He exhaled and blew the smoke toward the ceiling.

"It's about the tree. Don't you see?"

The veteran gave her back his full attention.

"How can it be about the tree if you want it girdled? It'll be a dead stump."

"Can't you see how loving something might cost you another thing you love? Like Abraham, for the love of God, was willing to sacrifice his son. I don't know—it's a long story."

"It's always a long story when what you're up to makes no sense. But, short or long, I damn well won't do it. Besides, what do you love big enough to kill Ghosthead Oak? Connect the dots for me."

"It *is* the tree that I love. Not the wood and the leaves of it. The *story* of Ghosthead Oak. Pages of my life are written into the story of the tree. My grandfather and my father, their lives—whole chapters' worth. If anybody could understand, I thought it might be you. I know where your uncle found you tied up back when that happened with your daddy."

Anger quickly rose in the veteran's eyes, but he took another long pull on his cigarette and it drifted away like so much smoke. "That—" he paused, "that happened a long time ago. It's nothing to you."

"Everybody talked about it. And then you didn't come back to school."

"We moved."

"And you've moved back here, again," she said. Then, quietly, a question. "Maybe we should both turn loose the tree. Maybe we can save the story of the tree if it does not become the game warden's toy."

"Maybe you go have another glass of wine and calm down a minute."

The widow stood and brushed her jacket front. She told him, "I'm sorry I troubled you."

"Troubled me? That's one way of putting it," the veteran said.

She said nothing, only closed her jacket tighter with her fist when she stepped out the tiny door into the edge of night. She left the door open. When he got up to close the door he saw the ax still tilted against the trailer.

"You might want to shoulder this thing," the veteran called out. "That cat's still out there somewhere."

The widow stopped, her long hair spilling down her back. She turned partway around. In the twilight shadows, the hem of her pale dress swaying as she turned, she could have been a billowy wraith from his childhood dreams.

"What is out there is something wild. Whatever the outcome, I'm in league with it. And so are you," the widow said. "You keep the ax."

THE WIDOW REACHED DOWN HER GRANDFATHER'S
journal from its place on the shelf above her small desk.
She sat in the cane-bottomed chair, keeping the rubbed
and worn book on her lap, her hand atop its oily leather
binding. She bent forward slightly, her fingers on her knee.
She moved her fingers down the outside of her calf to the
cut where she traced its crescent shape. She had cleaned the
wound, but she had not yet applied a bandage and thought
perhaps she would not unless it started to bleed again. It had
been a glancing blow from the ax and was not very deep.

She sat up and gazed through the dusty windowpane
at the darkness, how it encroached onto her porch from all
its dominion out there. Just this house, the big tree, and the
little distance between them were the metes and bounds of
her world and held the ebb and flow of her thoughts. The
rest of her hundred acres was under the purview of the
moon and stars, and tomorrow's sun, and always the wind
and rain and bees and goats and wildcats and snakes and

all manner of creatures, their watchful eyes blinking in ambivalence.

But I am done with looking-on, she thought. And when the words had formed in her mind she opened the journal to set them down in pencil. Her grandfather wrote only on right-reading pages, a quirk which left the facing page blank for her *notions*, as she thought of her own simple writing in comparison to the eloquence of her grandfather's.

When those years ago—following her husband's death— she had given herself permission to add to the journal, she also decided to write in pencil. For two reasons: One, her father only used pencils. He had once shown her thirty-year-old penciled notations in his hour and labor books. "See how the writing lasts," he'd said. He had likewise pointed out to her marginal notes in pre-Civil War volumes he took from his shelves.

"But, Father," she had said, "the words can be erased."

"And, then, if one so wishes they should be erased," he had answered. And that was the second reason: there might come a day when the lines she wrote would seem to her silly or untrue and she would erase them.

She switched on the desk lamp, its yellow wash of light obscuring the night outside the window and illuminating her dim corner. She opened the journal and found the page where her grandfather described the end of Ghosthead Oak in cryptic phrases about blood and water. From the narrow top drawer she drew out a pale green pencil, one of more than a hundred advertising pencils her father had collected. Some round, some hexagonal, even some flat carpenter pencils: GASTON FORD, STAR FISH AND OYSTER, FAIRHOPE COURIER, EVINRUDE OUTBOARD MOTORS.

Some of the pencils were unsharpened. The ones with points got them from a pocketknife and not a grinder, as her father had referred to mechanical sharpeners. "That contraption is just a Yankee trick to eat up pencils more quickly," he'd said.

The widow crooked her left forearm on the desk, inclined forward over the open journal and wrote: *Those days have come.* She underlined the four words. Her fingers trembled, and then she began again, writing in a measured and rhythmic hand. *Nature doesn't care*, she put. *She doesn't need for us to save her. Her ways don't need fixing. If we make a big cold gray mess of the world, in a thousand or a million years some dead seed will crack open, bend a root downward, and push a green and growing face up toward the sun to see what it has come back to.*

The widow pushed back for a moment and closed her eyes. There in her mind she could see Ghosthead Oak a quarter mile away, its jade green leaves shaking in the cold December wind, lord of the night and centuries past.

She wrote again.

Blood and water, one and the other both wet and moving. Warm and red. Cold and silver. She blinked, and shut the book and got up from the desk. She walked over to the

fireplace and took the cast iron poker from the tall milk can
her father had designated as the keeping place for fireplace
utensils. She poked at the coals and rearranged the logs until
flames sprang to life and she watched their silky movements,
staring at the fire until the years wavered and she was a child
again, a girl of nine or ten. She had been on an outing with
her father when he stopped his pickup on the shoulder of
River Road near Ghosthead Oak.

"I got something to show you," he had said.

Her father pointed into the bed of the truck.

"That box in the corner, in it's a clean bucket with a lid
on it," he said. "Get it and come with me."

The girl scrambled into the back of the dusty black
Ford, and, in a box pinched into the corner of the bed by
a bale of green hay, among four one-gallon glass jugs, was
a shiny new bucket with a lid clamped on. She snagged it
and hopped to the ground. She took off after her father, who
was already going out of sight down a narrow path into a
huckleberry thicket set in a scattering of palmetto palms.
The girl swung the jug in her left hand and brushed back the
spiky fan-shaped leaves of the palmettos with her right.

"Are we going to the big tree, Papa?"

The man grinned over his shoulder.

"Why do we need a bucket?" she asked.

Her father said nothing. The girl looked at his square
shoulders and straight back underneath a sweat-stained
khaki shirt. She would stand with her Papa and fight the

whole Union Army if they came charging out of the brush.

It was something to think about, for that's what they had done, the blue-coated soldiers, and they might come again to finish what they had started. Her father told her more than once how many had been shot and killed in Yankee raids. But the girl and her father could beat anybody. Or snakes. Or something with the rabies. She knew it, and would follow her Papa anywhere.

"What're we looking for, Papa?"

"We're not looking. I know right where it is, and so do you. It's something good," is all he said. Then, thirty steps farther, he told her, "Better watch for sand spurs."

"I can step right on 'em, Papa," the girl said. "My shoes've been under the bed since school let out."

"Yep, I expect they have," he said. He was grinning, but not so the girl could see.

The girl followed her father into the shade of the big tree. They stopped and became quiet. The girl reached for her father's hand and they stood side by side regarding the sheer size of the trunk. Many years later, stepping behind her husband into the aisle of his St. Mary's Church, she would be struck with the memory of that moment with her father, how her husband paused before going forward to communion, how he bowed his head before the cross in the sanctuary.

The girl allowed her eye to wander along the length of a low-swooping branch, thicker through than her father's horse at its chest, how the sun fell in drops onto the leaves, how the branch went out there a hundred feet and twisted upward at the end as if reaching for something.

"Come up here and stand," her father said. "Give me the bucket. You hold onto the lid. Now, mind, you be very quiet."

She watched him take a pipe and cloth pouch from his shirt pocket and tamp the pipe's bowl full of tobacco. He took a match from his britches and flicked its head with his thumbnail and lit his pipe and pulled deeply, puffing out thick smoke. The toasty apple smell drifted to the girl and she inhaled and closed her eyes. Her father turned and waved at her with the stem of his pipe, giving her a wink and a smile.

"Now, watch Papa," he said.

She had no idea what he was about to do and cocked her head to the side the way a puppy might when he stopped at a white-barked tree in the mid-morning sun. He took his pipe into his mouth and puffed up his cheeks with smoke and bent as if to kiss the tree. He put his mouth to a hole and exhaled. Tendrils of smoke escaped into the air around his face, but most of it poured into the hole and drifted out of a larger dark hole just at shoulder height. He clinched the pipe with his teeth and stood upright.

That's when she detected the bee. Then another, and another flying around her father's head. He stood up, took another pull on his pipe and repeated the kiss and puff. More bees looped around him.

With his left hand holding the bucket close to the bigger hole, he reached in with his right and extracted something. A clump of something that dripped amber honey. He turned over his hand and let it fall into the bucket. Then he took another wad and plopped it into the bucket. Then a third.

Her father turned, pipe still hanging in his mouth, and walked toward her. His hand was sticky with honey. He handed the bucket to her, took his pipe into his left hand and licked his fingers.

"Have a taste from in there," he said, pointing with the stem of his pipe, "then put on the lid."

Her eyes and her smile were wide as she curled her pointer into the bucket. "That's a honeycomb," she told him, and he nodded. She was about to taste the honey on the tip of her finger when she got a quizzical look on her face. She held her finger up, honey dripping, and asked, "Why didn't the bees sting you, Papa?"

"Because they weren't afraid of me, child," he said. "Plus" —and he gave her a big wink—"I made them just a little bit sleepy with the smoke. There's a way to work with the bees, and even mean old snakes, where we don't get bit."

"What way, Papa? With a pipe? Can you blow smoke on a copperhead? What work do we do with snakes?"

Her father filled the space underneath the oak tree with a laugh big enough to overflow all the way to Weeks Bay.

"No, ma'am. You cannot blow smoke in a snake's face. But you can give him some respect. He's not looking for your fear. Give a copperhead some respect and you can do the work of walking past him without getting bit."

"What kind of respect, Papa?"

"Room. Just don't crowd him and he'll let you be. I'll never need to cut Xs into your skin."

"But, Papa, snakes are sneaky."

"No, honey, a snake just travels low to the ground and that makes him look kind of sneaky. All God's critters got ways you can understand. And you will, honey. You'll grow into it natural. Wait and see, it's kind of in your blood."

And tonight, her eyes blurring from the heat of the fire, her blood pulsed toward his memory, flowed red into her own fading dreams. *It's kind of in your blood.* And the widow wondered about talk of destiny, of prophecy, of blood rights and blood duties. All the words in her head gave her little comfort when she seemed to stand alone against people and ways she could not understand.

She walked back to her desk, sat down and wrote a line:
The time has come.

The widow's dog came and stood beside her, its tail thumping the wall near the window. The gauzy curtain that hung to the floor stirred as if set into motion by the swinging tail, but there might have been other currents moving about in the room. She rubbed her dog's head. Then she wrote:

Something new waits to grow from the salty dark earth.

And she opened the drawer and put away the pencil. She closed her grandfather's journal and placed it carefully in the center of the desk, switched off the lamp and went to bed. The widow's dog took her place, curled on a rug by the front door, listening to the night where silent stars kept watch.

THE GAME WARDEN LOVED TO HOLD FORTH ABOUT GHOSTHEAD Oak when there was an audience at Miss Loo's riverside store and bait shop. Two men, or three—fishermen all—would do for his congregation, though sometimes half a dozen or more would lean against a post or wall, or squat while the officer rambled on about the big oak, how it was a national treasure.

"Up to me," he said, and he might here put his hand on his gun, adjust his hat, "I'd get that damn fence down and pave a road in there so folks could take a gander at the King Kong of oak trees."

Such talk caught in the craw of some, and those would narrow their eyes in his direction. Others waved him off saying, "It's the widow's land. Period. Hers to do with as she would. Hell, you want to go in there and look at that old tree, then just go." Others paid the game warden no mind.

When the game warden's audience waned, or his boat's VHF radio squawked, he would pay for his Pepsi and his Slim

Jim sausage stick and cross the dock, untie his all-business dark green aluminum boat and fire up the twin Yamaha outboards. He was the kind of man, with an attitude of authority and a loud, deep voice, that some might expect to make good show of his exit in a spray of water and surging wake. But the game warden always held idle speed until past the first channel buoy marking the way into the shallows of Weeks Bay. Even then, he'd ease the boat onto a plane and continue down the channel at three-quarters throttle.

On this morning the stop-off at Miss Loo's had been brief for the game warden and his deputy. A quick cup of coffee. Small talk about the upcoming shrimping season off Big Mouth and south Mobile Bay. The game warden and his deputy left by the side door, jumped into the workboat and tossed off dock lines fore and aft.

"Can I drive the boat?" the deputy wanted to know.

"No, and you might want to put on the foul weather jacket in that locker there."

"Is it going to rain?"

"No," the game warden answered, "only cold as a witch's tit."

The deputy took out a heavy yellow slicker and zipped up, gripped one of the aluminum stanchions holding up a small canvas top over the controls console.

"Ready," he said.

"Then I'll show you some of our beat."

The deputy said, "Help me get a feel for what's out here."

"All in the job description," the game warden said.

The bow of the boat rose with the thrust of the twin engines, then settled onto a plane. The hull's deep vee cut easily through the chop, though the aluminum was noisy in response to the water and waves. The wind was frigid, like a slap to the cheeks, pinching their skin, reddening their ears.

The game warden pulled back on the throttle and the bow settled low as the boat slowed. "That house right there, and that one three doors down," he said, "is where a crew of river bandits guzzle beer and sleep by day waiting to work their dark magic under cover of night."

While the boat eased along, their gaze followed an osprey flying with a fat fish caught in its talons, the catch of the day held longwise to cut down on wind resistance.

The deputy said, "So, you think the widow's tree ought to be open to the public?"

"It's not her tree," he said. "Who can own something like that, some green and growing thing like that? Biggest goddamn tree on the coast. Be like some redneck cowboy holding a deed to the Grand Canyon. Bullshit."

"I'll tell you what I've not yet told another soul," he went on. The game warden cut the throttle and gripped the steering wheel with both hands, tensing his jaw. "So, I knock on the widow's door last fall and ask her to sell me three acres. Enough, I said, to run one of those split-rail fences around Ghosthead Oak and have a paved road and a parking lot. So folks can get at the tree, you know. I stand right there on her porch sipping a Pepsi while she tells me, Thank you, but no part of my place is for sale."

The game warden paused, remembering the soda pop he'd set in the drink holder. He took a swallow and lowered the can and stood quiet for a moment, staring at the pop-top opening.

"Such a thing as that tree has become, I tell her, puts it in the category of public use. Tell her there's such a thing as eminent domain. I look her right in her baby blues and tell her she might want to learn something about that. She's a real pretty woman, you know." He looked puzzled. "Damn if I can remember what color her eyes are. 'Baby blues' is just a saying, I guess you know. Anyhow, I can tell you right then she had a mean and lost look about her."

The game warden continued. "Then she tells me things can go mighty wrong trying to take things from people by force. Woman lowers her voice, and says, 'A chapter and verse you might have missed, sir.' That's how she puts it. 'You might want to study that, officer, sir,' she tells me. Then she steps back and closes her door. You believe that? Sounded like a threat to me. Doesn't leave a reasonable man very many options."

The game warden steered around a log floating in the river.

"I didn't even see that," the deputy said.

"Not the passenger's job to," the game warden said.

The deputy asked, "So what did you do then?"

"Well, her gangly-legged black dog jumps on the porch and stares at me until I make to go. Then the hound follows right on my heels as I go. I mash my drink can into a wad and toss it at the thing. Get the hell back away, I tell the dog. Then it stops and the hair on its back pinches up into a narrow ridge along its spine. I know when its tail drops and hangs there still, it wants to bite me."

"So I walk slowly across the yard to my pickup, open the door and reach inside, take out another Pepsi from my little cooler on the seat. I pop it open, take a long pull, and turn toward the widow's cottage. No way she could've heard me, but I say soft-like in her direction, You've not heard the last from me on this."

The game warden pulled back on the throttle, bringing the boat to a quick standstill in the river. The deputy lurched forward, but held on. "See if you can get this idea to gel in your head. A boy can cobble together a clubhouse in a tree, a woman can water and prune a tree in her yard, a carpenter can build a table with boards cut from a tree, a family can gather in front of a fireplace blazing with sawlogs. But for someone to say, This is *my* tree—"

The game warden's voice trailed off, as though a new thought were springing up that he must attend to or lose it for all time.

"Well," said the deputy, "it does have the ring of a flawed principle." He squeezed his collar in his right fist, gave an exaggerated shiver. Both men were quiet, and where their shoulders had been near to touching as they talked above the outboards, now they shifted apart. Then the deputy drew back in quickly.

"You know what it is? It just hit me. What's the difference if the state claims the tree and throws up a chain link fence instead of the widow's barbed wire fence? Stations a ranger on the gate. Locks it down at dusk." He pulled in even closer to the game warden.

"It's a hell of a difference," the game warden said. "She's one person. The state's all of us."

The deputy said, "Yeah, but I'm thinking of the time Indians were offered a Federal deed to some land down the road from their ancestral home. The chief asked the big bellies in Washington how a man can take title to his mother."

"Oh, hell," the game warden said. "Let's stop and hug that cypress over there on the bank."

"I actually hugged a tree once in an English class," the deputy said.

"I don't doubt it," the game warden said.

"The professor took us outside and lined us up in front of a magnolia on campus. We hugged. We meditated. We wrote a poem about the experience."

"That was in the great city of Tuscaloosa no doubt," the game warden said. "But, enough of that crap. I'm going to show you another local treasure, writer boy. This one lives and breathes and is crazy as a run-over dog. Maybe crazier than the widow."

He pushed the throttle forward slowly and aimed the boat upstream in Magnolia River and followed its winding course for a good three miles, then swung off into Buzzard Creek. Aptly named, for the deputy counted five of the gangly birds standing tall in someone's boathouse, and another pair actually inside the boat on its hoist. "That's kind of Gothic-looking. A little spooky." Then the deputy asked if a feature had been done on the birds.

The game warden cut the throttle.

"About fifty times," the game warden said with some disdain, then brightened and pointed across the port bow. "Astute fellow like you been noticing the mailboxes on dock pilings along this river?"

"I have taken heed of them, yes."

"Well, take heed of this. It's the last place in America where mail is delivered by boat. No doubt you find that quaint. Right? Another story been done to death. But, now if I get soft-hearted and approve you to moonlight stories—"

"I told you," the deputy said, "I'm done with reporting."

"Sure thing, writer boy," the game warden said. "Now, cut your keen eye over there to the name on that mailbox."

"Jezzabelle Sweet?"

"That's her."

"A made-up name?"

"Ain't yours? Fathers and mothers go out and hug a tree and get on a tear to be creative, or properly respectful of family names. They're all made up, writer boy. Think a minute. But this Jezzabelle is the real deal. You'll see."

The deputy asked, "She another one of your armed hermits?"

"Oh, no. Jezzabelle gets around. She's no hermit. Didn't you see her 14-foot jon boat with that nice Evinrude? Hanging in her boatlift back there. You need to pay more attention, writer boy. She shows up at Miss Loo's two, three times a week."

The game warden nosed the boat to a dilapidated pier, and the two men tied up the boat. The deputy followed the game warden along a trail that looked appropriated from a jungle in some South American rainforest. "Watch for moccasins," the game warden said over his shoulder.

"Nice try, boss. I know snakes are dug in for the winter." The deputy stopped. "But, now, what kind of bird is that?" In the distance, a loud double-pitched trill.

"I look like a bird watcher?" the game warden asked.

"Just thought it would be part of your job to know the local game."

"Oh, I know the game. So well I can play it in my sleep."

"That's not what I—"

"Home sweet home," the game warden said as they came into a clearing ringed with lush palmetto palms and sword ferns and ivy heavy on tangled bushes, enough green to make a man long for a change of seasons. A screen door on the tilted porch swung open and out of the ramshackle hovel came a coffee-skinned woman of indeterminate age and race, skinny as a wire, toothless as a pocket. Gray and black hair all over the place, it looked like it hadn't been combed in weeks. She wore a long cotton dress, the color long since poured out in the wash water. The garment hung loose and low on her chest, and she topped it off with a new-looking denim jacket. Black lace-up shoes and no socks finished off her wardrobe. The witchy-looking woman tossed up her hand.

"Mister Law," she said, in a voice like fingernails on a blackboard. Was she grinning? Her eyes were black, rheumy in the corners.

"Wanted you to meet my new deputy, Jezzabelle."

She curtsied and nodded.

"He's a mighty purty boy, that one," she said. "You want to leave him with me. I got work needs doing around my ranch here."

"I better keep him, I guess. At least for now. But you know, I don't pay him much, and he might need to borrow a dollar. You got one to loan?" The game warden gave a sidelong look at the deputy, who calculated something was up: the two were in cahoots and had just exchanged some signal.

The emaciated woman on the porch bent to the floor and grabbed the hem of her threadbare dress. She stood and flipped it up to her chest exposing her privates to the men. Tied around her waist was an old nylon stocking, and the toe of it bulged and dangled heavily. She untied the stocking and snaked her bony arm inside it to withdraw a wad of bills. She chose a single, and then lifted her dress to retie her ersatz money belt.

"What you thank, mister man?" She held up the dollar. "I always got a dollar for my brothers and sisters in need. 'As why they calls me sweet, I reckon." For a moment, the woman made no move to drop her dress.

"Oh, my God," the deputy cried, turning his head, stunned. Which seemed to completely satisfy the game warden. He and the woman on the porch laughed in voices that sounded like a mix of yelling and strangling. When composure, in sufficient measure, settled on the pair, the crone tilted her head forward and burned a brown eye toward the game warden. Her demeanor shifted entirely. Her mouth worked as if she were chewing a cud, and she seemed to take over.

"Now, you done come up in here all foolish and such, Mister Law. But Jezzabelle gone tell you she sees something dark an' heavy 'round you. You talkin' lots but you ain't tellin' all."

Now the game warden took a U-turn and a fire caught in his eyes and his features grew hard and locked down.

"Show's over," he said. "Time to shut up and get on back in there with the rats and chickens. About-face, writer boy. I think I hear the VHF calling."

The game warden actually dropped his hand on the deputy's shoulders, as if to turn him around and head him back down the trail toward the boat.

"What the hell?" the deputy said.

"Like I said, one crazy-ass loon. We came, we saw, we're gone. Come on. Let's move."

"What kind of fortuneteller mumbojumbo was that? What's she mean, you're talking and not telling all?"

"No meaning exists in that woman's head. Not a speck," the game warden said. "Just step it up and let's get moving. We've lollygagged around enough this morning."

THE VETERAN WATCHED THE ANNOUNCEMENT OF SUNSET growing in the western sky. Gray cirrus tinged orange and pink with swatches of deep blue showing through here and there, dark bundles of cumulus closer to the horizon. He stood on his dock, a bucket at his feet. His cast net was bundled inside it.

He took one long last drag on his cigarette and lifted his boot, crushing it out against the sole and dropping the butt into his shirt pocket. A sporty fishing boat raced into view around the bend, its console t-top decorated with red and green Christmas lights. The driver spied him on the dock and gave a goofy grin and an animated wave. The veteran guessed the boater might have a beer close at hand and watched him speed down the middle of the river until he caught another bend and was out of sight.

The veteran reached into the bucket and found the end of the net's lead line, slipped the noose over his left wrist and withdrew the coil of filament in big loops. Using a technique his uncle had taught him, he gathered the net into his hands for the toss. He moved out to the end of the finger pier and stood watching the water for the flash of a mullet's shiny scales. They traveled in schools, and a good haul would be breakfast and lunch tomorrow. The veteran's father had detested the fish, saying it was *going off* even as river water still dripped from its sides, and that was mostly true. Mullet had to be carefully kept until cooked and never tasted good refrigerated for more than a day before frying. Sometimes, the veteran would smoke mullet fillets all day over pecan logs and that way have the salty meat on hand indefinitely without having to cook.

He stood for almost five minutes, completely still, the net poised and ready. His breath fogged the chilly evening air. The quiet lured him to thoughts of the widow. He saw her hazel eyes, her fair face—the freckles, her jet black hair… all in juxtaposition with blazing worry and frustration. It spoiled her eyes, he remembered thinking that when she sat at his table. He reckoned some push to take *his* land would be met with violence. Plain and simple. The veteran knew bureaucrats, and he had only contempt for the *gub'mint* his father had lambasted from one side of his mouth while working the other in favor of the Army.

He instinctively gripped the net harder, recalled his dealings with the VA hospital over in Biloxi. A big orderly had stepped from behind the counter, summoned on some slight signal from the receptionist. *Sir! Step away from the counter.* And he had looked at one and then the other. When he reached into his pants pocket for his ID, the big man cocked his arms and made a quick move toward the veteran. The veteran had stepped back, flicked the ID on the counter in front of the woman. "When you get your paperwork in order," he said to her in a measured voice, "drop me a line."

He flexed his bicep, feeling a little burn from the weight of the net.

Then he saw five, six, or more mullet swimming toward him.

When he made a half-turn with his torso, the fish darted left and away in the direction they'd come from. Within a minute they were back and he gave a twist and tossed the net. It struck the water round as the moon, a sixteen-foot circle of monofilament dropping toward the muddy bottom of the river as fast as the lead weights at its circumference would drag it downward. When the veteran tugged on the lead line he felt the weight of fish bundled into the net, felt the electric tremble of the line. He nodded as he pulled the net in and lifted it onto the boards of the pier. He'd caught four fat fish.

He moved to the broader floor of the boathouse and shook the fish onto the boards. Each flopped a time or two, and then lay still while he hung the net on a nail and leaned over the dock and got water in the net bucket. The veteran picked up the fish and dropped them into the water, took the bail of the bucket and lifted it for the short stroll up the hill to his trailer. He'd clean and filet the fish on a juniper stump he sawed off waist-high just for that purpose after a hurricane last year broke the top out of the tree. It was far enough from the trailer so the scent of fish blood and guts didn't bother him.

Behind him, a squawk sounded from close range. He turned his head, and dancing side-to-side on an old piling in shallow water beside the boathouse was a crow. Its yellow beak was open.

"What's up, pal?" The veteran smiled, addressing the bird. "You looking for supper?"

The crow bobbed its head up and down and cawed again.

"Then you gotta follow me. We're taking this work home."

The veteran walked toward the Airstream, half expecting the bird to follow him. But as he stood at the juniper stump, whetting the filet knife, the woods all around him were still and quiet. Only the widow was there, moving, evanescent— an echo, really— disturbing the silence.

GAME WARDEN SEEKS PARK FOR BIG TREE
Special to the Gazette

A local game warden, working through the baldwin county commission office, filed a petition before state officials seeking to appropriate three acres of land by right of eminent domain, when the owner refused to sell to a citizens' group headed by the game warden. The reason for the move, according to a spokesperson for the commission office, is to establish a state park for public access to a champion live oak tree known within the area as Ghosthead Oak.

THE DEPUTY SCANNED THE REST OF THE BRIEF ARTICLE, tucked away inside the newspaper on page three. He sat with his feet propped on the game warden's desk. The boss was away in Montgomery, probably advancing a little further this cause of eminent domain.

He kept staring at the page, though his mind had moved on to three things of note. One, Special to the Gazette meant someone who was not a reporter on staff at the newspaper filed the story. He could detect a tone to the piece, certain to be the work of a PR writer. Two, a touch of irony: the photo of the tree was taken by someone trespassing on the widow's land, since there was no suitable vantage point from the road for taking pictures of Ghosthead Oak. And, three: the deputy wondered which of the game warden's cronies might be on the roster of the citizens' group?

The deputy got up, walked out of his office and down the hall. He had no duties or instructions to the contrary, so he was going for a boat ride. On the wall near the front door was a board cut in the rough shape of an alligator, with a row of hooks where keys to equipment hung. He picked out a boat key ring and grabbed his hat from another peg.

It should be easy enough, he thought, to find his way back to Jezzabelle Sweet's place. It would not be easy, however, to take up questions with her. He would just make the trip and see what happened. His hippie friend at the *Tribune* had chided him, "Stop *appropriating*, brother, just *allow*. It's like letting, not grabbing. It works. Try it, you'll see that what comes of its own accord is better than what's taken."

So, he'd try it. See what good things come to those who wait. Any way I cut it, he thought, it won't be boring.

Instead of the big aluminum vee-bottom boat, the game warden's baby, the deputy opted for the old Boston Whaler, a 17-foot Montauk model outfitted with a 4-stroke Yamaha, like the bigger boat. A good dependable boat with enough nicks and scrapes—what the fishermen called piling rash—so that he wasn't too concerned with his limited skills. He'd risk it for one more shot at the voodoo queen, to hear one more chorus of her song about the game warden.

Walking down the dock toward the boat, some reporter blood filtered into his brain: Jezzabelle Sweet, for sure a story that had not been done. And he found himself wondering where he could freelance such a piece. He found himself missing his desk, cranking out a story, sweating the minutes toward an editor's deadline.

The wind was low, and the sun warmed the December Tuesday morning. The outboard started first click and he untied the boat and eased it out of the slip. He set the bow toward the middle of the river. The water was flat and slick, no other boats in sight. The deputy immediately felt at home in the Whaler. He liked the old mahogany seats and center console, the *verdigris* patina on the brass fittings. The engine was quiet enough that he actually heard the whistle of an osprey and scanned the tree-lined riverbank to port, then to starboard, spotting the osprey just as it settled into an unruly assortment of twigs and branches at the top of a tall, dead pine tree.

The deputy cruised along, watched mullet jumping, heard the rattling call of a kingfisher, saw it hovering then plunging into the river, missing its prize. He ticked off names on the dock-mounted mailboxes, thinking of the untold zigzag miles a mailman would have to cover down little lanes and side trails to deliver a single letter, some bill or magazine, and how the river route made perfect sense.

He cut back on the throttle and slipped into the mouth of Buzzard Creek. He watched for the name Jezzabelle Sweet, thought he must be getting close. Had he missed it? He slowed the Whaler, looked over his shoulder and scanned the few docks he'd passed. Then, peering ahead, he spotted her boat, tied alongside the finger pier instead of hanging in the lift. Either she had made an outing, or she was getting ready for one.

He eased the bow of the boat against the dock, bumping into a wobbly piling. The deputy gained his balance and went forward to make the boat fast with the line coiled on the foredeck for that purpose. He moved aft to tie the stern and was bent to his task when Jezzabelle startled him.

"What you doin' out in the swampland, Mister Deputy?"

She carried a small red plastic gas can and wore rolled-up jeans and rubber sandals. If he had wondered would her feet not get cold, one look at the tough, cracked skin below her ankles gave him the answer. She raked her fingers through her hair and then propped a hand on her hip, waiting for his answer.

"It's not official business," the deputy offered.

"No concern by me," she said. "I'm too damn old to worry over such trifles."

"Well, I, ah— I was just curious about what you said the other day. That thing about talking a lot and not telling all. Maybe you know the game warden's asked the state to take the widow's land for public use."

"My ass," she said. "Ain't nothin' public 'bout they reasons to steal that piece of land from that woman."

"So, I'm thinking my head would roll if the boss knew I was asking you this, but I wonder what those other reasons might be."

"Sho you do. Prolly lots of other folks wants to know, too. But I ain't tellin' nothin'."

"But why would you poke at the game warden, what you said and all, if you have nothing else to say about it?"

"Who was I talkin' to? Oh, you pretty boy."

"Well—him."

"Not you?"

"No, ma'am."

"Oh, now you say *ma'am* to ol' Jezzabelle. I done caught you out. 'Member how them boys on the schoolyard would say it to you? Get up in yo' face. *I ain't talkin' to you.*"

The deputy grinned. "It's been said to me. Maybe a month ago. Ex-girlfriend."

"I'll be yo' sweetie pie, Mr. Deputy. But I ain't said nothin' to *you* about Mister Law. Better go ask yo' boss, you want to know something about what he's up to."

"Do you know what?" the deputy said.

"Yeah," she answered. "But it's for me to know and you

to find out." She spat into the water and cackled.

"Yes, ma'am. What I can do is get back in my boat. Ease out of this creek. Anything I need to know will find its way to me."

"Well, it damn sho will. You smarter than I reckoned. An' here Jezzabelle thinkin' you nothin' but a pretty face. I ain't looked at a newspaper or the TV or turned on the radio in forty years an' I bet I know all I need to know. Hurricane comin'? Somebody tell me. Politician caught lyin' and cheatin'? That's done some old news anyway. House catch on fire? I don't want to hear it."

"Sort of like that man I saw back down the river," the deputy said, hooking his thumb over his shoulder. "He was dancing around on his dock swatting at something, maybe a bee. Thought he'd fall in for sure. I wanted to pull over and tell him to stand still. Let the bug come to him. Get right in his line of fire in no time."

"Now then, think a minute," Jezzabelle said. "I done stirred up one bug a little. You jus' set and wait. See where it land."

The deputy touched his finger to his forehead, a kind of salute, and bent to undo the dockline.

"Before I go can I give you a hand there, Miss Jezzabelle?"

"No, boy. You keep dat hand for yo'self. You might need it." Jezzabelle spat. "I tell you this, though. Some folks got help like extra hands, you know."

"I'm sorry, Miss Jezabelle. I don't know what—"

"This is what. Dem Indians calls a big cat *too la dah chee*. That means protector. You hear me? Somebody in dis mess got a protecting hand. Mister Law, he don't b'lieve the cat is here. It is. Big ol' black something."

"I believe there could be a panther. Yes, ma'am. That it's possible for one to be in this county, roaming the lowlands."

"Possible? Boy, if Jezzabelle say a chicken dip snuff, lif' up its wing and find the snuff can." She shook her head, as if reaching for someone not capable of grasping the hand offered. "Listen. Indians calls a crow *go guh*. One that sees. And that widow, she got a raven's heart and eyes to see. Stuff to study, pretty boy. Don't mess up."

And the deputy calculated there was a mess to be made if all were not careful.

N THE PARKING LOT AT THE NEPTUNE CLUB FOUR MILES East on Pensacola Highway, the widow found mostly pickup trucks. It was 5:30 Thursday afternoon and these were workingmen who grabbed a beer before going home, though she guessed some would still be here at closing time.

She eased her '82 Volvo station wagon between a red Chevy Silverado and a tiny four-door Hyundai, one of only two cars on hand. The Volvo had been her husband's pride and joy. He called it a lawyer's professor car. It was pretty good on gas, and she'd kept the tires rotated and the oil changed and the fuel tank full and had never thought to get another automobile. It was still dependable today, if only a little faded.

The widow switched off the engine, but before opening her door, sat a minute with both hands on the wheel. She took a deep breath and exhaled slowly. Then she got out and went inside the dark tavern, waiting by the door until her eyes adjusted to the dim light. Every man in the room looked at her. Over in the corner, a three-foot-high stack of beer cans hot-glued in concentric circles passed for a Christmas tree. It was adorned with so many strings of lights the cans were all but obscured. A single clear long-neck bottle sat atop the creation. The widow took her eyes from the tree and spoke right up.

"Is there one of you who knows how to operate a chainsaw?"

Her voice was too loud, she assessed, but held it there and added, "Who wants to make three hundred dollars?" She had not really known what to expect in response, but at least one scenario in her head featured every man jumping from his barstool or table and lining up in front of her to interview for whatever job she offered.

No one stirred. No one spoke. These men had just quit a long workday, she suddenly realized, and talking about more work was likely the last thing they wanted to do. Maybe she should turn and go. Right away. Her heart began to beat fast. She blinked, couldn't move.

"What ye got in mind, girlie?" The voice came from a chair at a table off to the right, over by an unplugged 1950s Wurlitzer jukebox. It startled her though several steps away.

Then, as the mind will sometimes do, she was momentarily distracted from her frightening mission, chasing off down a frivolous rabbit trail. She'd been called *girlie*. She surmised the man there in the darkness was someone up there in years himself.

"Ah, I—" she said, hesitating. The widow was not at all willing to broadcast to the room at large the nature of the work she proposed, only willing in that manner to seek interested parties. She was about to home in on the table where the voice had come from, when a man stepped from the low light and smoke and stood right in front of her.

He must have been seventy, was no more than five and a half feet tall, and not much over a hundred and twenty pounds, but a strap of rusty steel with a hawkish nose and gray stubble. His eyes were like black fire underneath heavy brows. The widow pictured him standing wide-legged aboard a tossing ship with a gold hoop earring and a razorsharp cutlass in his belt, cursing the wind to lie down.

"I got my steel in the bed of my truck, locked up in my toolbox," the little pirate said. "You got cash?"

"Yes, sir. I have the money to pay for the work when it's done."

"Show me," he said.

"Excuse me?"

"Show me the goddam money, or I set my happy ass back down and order me another beer."

The widow reached into the breast pocket of her jacket and produced a white envelope, opened it and took out three one hundred dollar bills, put them quickly back, and tucked away the envelope.

"May we please go outside?"

"Wherever you like."

The widow stepped outside the bar, into a wash of neon. She walked down to stand in front of the hood of her Volvo, as if it might take up for her should something go wrong in this meeting. She cleared her throat, mustered a matter-of-fact tone and told the man who'd followed her outside that she had a place down the road about five miles.

"On my land is a tree, a giant live oak. Too big to be cut down." Without further explanation, "I wish to have it girdled so that it will die. Cut a six-inch deep vee all the way around its base and earn the money I've offered."

"Show me," he said. "I'm in that GMC right over there."

"This is my car."

"I'm right on your tail, girlie."

She winced. He watched her until she put her hand on the door handle and then walked bowlegged to his truck of indeterminate color, dressed for battle with a big silver toolbox and a four-poster ladder rack. The widow expected a loud roar from an exhaust with a burned-out muffler but the pickup was quieter than her Volvo.

She pulled out onto a deserted highway in the direction of Weeks Bay and her land. Within ten minutes, she'd pulled off onto the side road the trespassers preferred and stopped in the spot where she imagined the game warden had stopped last week. There was a turnaround a bit farther on where others would sometimes park so they could sneak through the bushes and tall grass out to the tree. She got out and waited for the pirate. He joined her without a word, a fat yellow flashlight swinging in his hand as he came, and the two of them took the path toward Ghosthead Oak.

"You won't need the spotlight," she said. The December sun had set more than an hour ago and the light was frail but the path was easily followed.

"I'll be the judge of that."

When they drew underneath the big oak's canopy, and the man snapped on his heavy duty light, extending it outward like a weapon, the widow felt a wave of nausea and began to sweat though the night was cold.

The white beam drenched the trunk of Ghosthead Oak so that it didn't even look alive but might instead be some lunatic furrowed sculpture for a fairy tale play. She undid the top buttons of her bulky jacket. She had no understanding of what was happening inside her at this moment. It was a storm, an emotional cold front clashing with warmer, deeper feelings and buffeting her like a rag in the wind. She'd had it rough when her husband died, and her father, but this was not like those times. This was more akin to panic, to some version of a child's terror for the ghouls and goblins of the night, and a pain in her abdomen, like something twisting her gut, made her gasp.

"Big tree," the pirate-gnome said. "Probably take me an hour." He kept the light on the tree and looked sideways at the widow. "Some way I can get my truck up in here past your fence?" Then the pirate put the light on her, not in her face, but at her knees, which still blinded her.

"I reckon it might not even be your fence," he said. "Maybe this here's a neighbor's land. Somebody you want to get even with. But I don't rightly give a shit once I get that pack of C-notes."

Tears spilled down her face and made of the widow's eyes a mess of redness. Each breath was a soft moan.

"I'm ready to do the deal," he said. "I got me a converter plug in the back that'll power up my work lights. I don't care to make this trip again. What's it goin' to be, girlie?"

"Thirty yards past where we turned through the gate, the fence is down," she said. "You can drive your truck through there." The widow took out the envelope and handed it over. She spun around to leave, remembered there were four one hundred dollar bills in the packet. She'd shown him three, and he'd agreed to that price. She turned, thought to say something—but never mind.

"Sorta like a Judas moment, huh? Wish I had me a Kodak."

The pirate-gnome played his light around the tree trunk, up into the canopy, out a long branch. "Some big ass tree, all right," he hollered behind her, but she was gone. Then to himself: "Hell, a feller could carve him out a room in there and live in that thing."

A crow cawed way up in the top of the tree someplace, but the objection got caught on the wind and was spun away and shredded within a copse of nearby cypress and sweet bay trees and the business at hand kept to its course.

THE VETERAN WAS OUTSIDE HIS TRAILER, SITTING ON THE bench with his leg crossed, his elbow parked on top of a barn-red two-by-four picnic table. He had a small fire going in a shallow crater he'd ringed with an oddment of bricks and pieces of bricks. A cigarette in one hand, tossing kindling and twigs onto his fire with the other. A glass of JD sat on the table at his back. He was singing softly.

Chestnuts roasting on an open fire...

The veteran's voice was nice, melodious, without vibrato and it was on pitch. The flames flickered yellow and waves of warmth brushed his face. He leaned back against the tabletop, turning to pick up his glass of whiskey. He whistled part of the verse he'd been singing.

First it was the sputter and bark of a chainsaw that caused him to jerk his head around in the direction of Ghost-head Oak. Then it was the halo of fluorescent light above the treetops that brought him to his feet and the words *Sonofabitch!* out of his mouth.

The veteran was off in a tear. He ran as if in a dream, faster than a man could go on foot, the landscape morphing into a floodtide as he raced toward the tree. Reality shifted to some ripple in time that folded in on itself and spread out again, like concentric rings on melted glass. The night itself exploded into a black sky too deep to float even one star.

The veteran burst underneath the big tree moving at full tilt, some kind of a rebel yell war cry entwining with the high-revving drone of a two-cycle engine at redline. The tip of a chainsaw's bar sank into the trunk of Ghosthead Oak and silver knifelinks spun a blur of oak chips onto the steel-toed boots of a little man bowed over his work.

Ancient. Powerful. Mute.

The veteran's head, the thick bone of his skull, crashed into the brittle cage of the sawman's ribs and the air went out of him with a big *ooommph*. On some other day in his rooster-fight youth the sawman might have come round with the two-foot whirring blade of his Stihl and sliced off an arm or a leg to even up the score before going down. It did not happen on this December night a week shy of Christmas.

The man was down. His eyelids fluttered but he could not speak.

The chainsaw idled *pa-pa-papa-pa-pa* bottom-up in the dirt six feet away.

The veteran walked over, thumbed the kill switch on the chainsaw, and curled its handle into the fist of his right hand. In a blur that seemed ten steps or less, still in the echo of some surreal madness, he bounded onto the widow's porch and kicked her door.

A wasted woman, eyes wet and hollow, hair twisted and going everywhere, a woman who could hardly stand held onto the opening door. Her black dog snarled and advanced slowly until the veteran screamed at them both, something like the gargled oath of a drowning man, and threw the chainsaw into her parlor. The dog yelped and dodged the rolling, clunking mass of bright orange and black metal that reeked of exhaust.

"You better get that bastard to a doctor," the veteran said. "He left a light on for you."

AT FIRST LIGHT, THE GRAY REMAINS OF NIGHT LINGERED among morning shadows, and the crow, on the ground but with her wings raised, stood on a fallen chunk of wood from the big tree. A twisted piece of branch the size and length of a man's leg, lichened bark peeling away to reveal a pair of beetles tussling with some tiny prize. No wind yet stirred the December cold. Far off in the direction of the big bend in Fish River, a whippoorwill sang a plaintive refrain and was answered by the shrill boast of an osprey.

The crow had its eye on the rough blanket of granular yellow oak pieces torn from the big tree and scattered like shrapnel over the moist brown leaves. Without a breeze, a thin odor of oil and gasoline still hung about the spot. The one who came with the saw was gone, though wide tire tracks cut an arc through the grass and underbrush.

The crow cawed, loud and raucous. Brought its fat breast low, almost touching the leaves, and cawed again with her wings still outstretched. Her eyes were tiny yellow jewels of anger displayed in black velvet.

Then the crow spied the button. A pearlescent disc with a twist of frayed white thread still attached through one of the tiny holes at its center. She folded her wings to her side and walked in an awkward pitching and yawing gait to stand over the button, turning her head to focus on the find. The crow took the button into her beak and with a dip rose into the breaking day.

THE DEPUTY STEPPED DOWN FROM THE SCOUT. THE game warden was pulling into a spot beside him in the hard-packed shell parking lot.

"Miss Loo's sausage and biscuit breakfast is reason enough to live in these parts," the game warden said. "South Florida's got nothing like this to get a day started." He stopped, looking over at the deputy's vehicle. "That's a hell of a dent in your hood there. What happened?"

The deputy decided this would be a better day if he just didn't mention what had really happened. "Car wash damage," he said. "They're ordering a new hood for me." He was ready to join the other men who also got their morning's fat fix at the bait shop and washed it all down with strong coffee. "You buying?" he asked.

"No," the game warden said.

The narrow boardwalk around to the side door hung precariously over the water, damaged in the last big storm, but it was the game warden's ritual point of entry into Miss

Loo's, and no threat of falling into the cold river was enough to bring him through the front door of the bait shop, away from his habits.

"Morning," the game warden said to a man tying up his fourteen-foot wooden skiff. "That a '60s Stauter you got there?"

"That's right," the man said, not turning or rising to see whose voice it was, like a proper congregant ignoring late-comers finding their pews.

The deputy, following closely, almost walked into the game warden when he recognized the veteran and immed-iately determined the game warden had not seen the face of the man whose land he wanted to buy. In the fluster, he quickly wondered did the veteran even know the game warden? Surely they'd met at the bait house, at least that crossing of paths. The deputy hung back, remaining behind the game warden for a minute, trying to forecast how this might go.

"I figured maybe twenty-five, thirty years old," the game warden said, "judging by that early-model Johnson outboard you got there. You got it looking good." The fishing skiff had newly painted topsides and a Bristol-kept interior. The game warden abandoned the small talk and walked ahead to cast a weather eye toward the low western sky beyond the boat slips.

The deputy thought the veteran looked friendly enough this morning, if a little on the rough side. The man's damp hair hung around his collar and he had the makings of a black and white beard, too long for stubble but not yet long enough to brush and tame. An onshore wind swept across the bay and up the river, ripples and catspaws skittered in the protected water and whipped a mist that sprinkled the veteran's blue, Navy-issue peacoat.

"Need any help, Vet?" Someone called from the corner of the store inside a screened porch.

"Got it. Thanks."

"Coffee and a biscuit, then?"

"That's right," the man said, stepping off his boat. "This a drive-up now? Or you going to leave me come inside and warm a minute?"

"Piss off, mate," came the voice again. "Coffee will be in that mug of your'n. Still missin' the handle. Still ain't been washed in a year."

"Good," the veteran answered, and neatly coiled down the end of the line into concentric circles as easy as another man might drop the rope's tail into a messy heap. He looked up and caught sight of the deputy. There was only the slightest hesitation, no greeting, not even a nod. The game warden held open the door for the deputy. The veteran went inside by a front door.

There was a swirl of smells in the bait shop, but coffee took top honors. A close second was a choice between the cigar minnows and shrimp swimming in their holding tanks or the aroma of biscuits coming out of the charred oven over in the corner behind the counter. The game warden told the deputy the sausage was fried up in skillets before dawn, before the doors were unlocked to the fishermen.

"That's so nobody knows the brand of sausage Loo buys," the game warden said. "Everybody wants to think it's some hand-squeezed secret recipe, but it might be the cheapest crap at the Winn-Dixie store. Who knows? Nobody but Loo. It's just damn good tucked inside one of her hot biscuits."

The deputy leaned in closer. "That fellow from the boat outside…you know him?"

"You mean the one who won't sell me his damn land? Know *of* him, seen him plenty up and down the river and in this joint a couple times a month, but never shook his hand." The game warden looked hard at the deputy. "He didn't much blink to see you. You sure you made a call on him?"

"I did, and like I said, backed my butt right off his place, too." The deputy was surprised the game warden was paying attention, thought it the mark of a good lawman. He shifted the line of talk away from himself. "He seems to know the guy on the porch," the deputy said.

"I expect he does. The guy's a dishwasher here, yammers at the pelicans when nobody else is around." The game warden tilted his head, indicating the back of the room. "You see Jezzabelle sitting in the corner?"

"Where?" The deputy scanned the room.

"Hunkered down back there at the table in the corner with old Captain MacNee."

"Yes," the deputy said. "I do see her. You going over and say hello?"

· "Hell no," the game warden snapped. "Those relics ain't looking for me."

"She come in by boat? I didn't notice it tied up outside."

"Prob'ly not," the game warden said. "Too cold out. Reckon the captain gave her a ride in."

The game warden and the deputy stood side by side at the counter while Miss Loo wrapped a sausage and biscuit in waxed paper and handed it and a cup of coffee in a yellowed ceramic mug with a broken handle to the dishwasher who took the order to the end of the counter and served the veteran. The game warden cocked an eyebrow.

"Some folks don't wait in line, I guess," he said in the direction of the deputy, though the remark was clearly intended for the veteran. He'd spoken loudly enough to be heard by all seven or eight men standing or sitting around the room, some at table, others on bait boxes, and the pair seated in the corner.

The dishwasher looked toward the game warden. The veteran did not. Only took his coffee and biscuit and went outside onto the screened porch. He sat on top of a table and put his feet into a chair though the cold wind still kicked up a chop on Weeks Bay out past the mouth of Fish River.

"You'll get yours," Loo said, grinning. "You think that pistol on your hip cuts you any slack with me?"

"When my pistol cuts me slack," the game warden said,

"it's more than a cup of coffee at risk. Lots more."

"Sheeeit," one of the fishermen said. "They giving you bullets now?"

"Reckon you goin' to need a handful of ammo you take on the widow," said another man in a yellow rain slicker hunkered over his coffee at a tiny corner table. The man was twice as wide as the chair he sat in.

"Yeah," chimed someone else. "What the hell's that in the paper you gonna lead some kind of gov'ment takeover of the poor woman's land?"

It was interesting to the deputy how quickly the room had devolved into tension thick enough to hang a hook in. Doing a quick rewind, he wondered if all that was needed to get it started had been the game warden's one jibe in the veteran's direction. He decided pretty quickly, based on some barroom experiences, that a single glance is sometimes more than enough to take a gaggle of idle men off in some crazy direction.

"My deputy here knows the facts," the game warden said. "He can tell you there's a bigger story than you chuckleheads are comprehending."

The deputy quickly raised his hands as if in surrender to a mugger. He flashed a quick, nervous smile. "Whoa," he said, "I don't have a dog in this hunt. I'm not reporting this story, boss."

"Maybe you ought to, then," said the man in the slicker.

"Yessir, give a voice to us common men," said another.

"The widow ain't a man or common," the game warden said.

"Dang sure ain't," one said. "Best lookin' woman between here and Cozumel."

"You ain't been to Cozumel, you old fool," said a shrimper in whiter rubber boots.

"I been to wherever I say I've been," the man answered.

"Anybody in here been, by God, to Russia? That's where the goddamn Federalees takes what belongs to the people."

"The Federales are in Mexico, you idjit."

"You gonna be with them you don't watch your mouth."

At that moment a brassy peal, like thunder from a bell, rang through the bait shop, vibrating the walls. A calendar fell from its spot on the wall above the drink cooler. Three men cupped their hands over their ears.

"Hell fire! What did you go and hammer that goddamn bell for, Loo?" The man asking her bore a look of pure pain.

"Now, boys," Loo said. "You will all drink your coffee and eat your biscuits like men at the church social—"

"Then hand out the guns and knives," one of the men said, coughing around his joke. "More fighting goes on at my church than in ye saloon, Loo."

"Gilbert, you just used your last excuse to speak up in my establishment," said Loo. She still held aloft the ball peen hammer she'd smacked into the side of the antique ship's bell suspended above the counter. "Now," she said, "no more of this bull in here." She waggled the hammer for emphasis.

"More coffee, anyone?"

The veteran had stepped back inside, was holding his cup out to the dishwasher who took it and walked toward the coffee pot.

"Before we kneel and pray," said the old captain in the corner, "I got something needs sayin'." He pushed his chair back from the table but remained seated. Jezzabelle Sweet's face was lit with a toothless grin, but then she lowered her head and put her palm to the side of her face.

"You invited a bigger story to save us from our ignorance, there, game warden. I reckon I can ask you, then, why come you trying to buy a strip of land to connect up that Cromwell place to the river? It's come to me from a good source—"

And the captain, who would not make a good poker player, let his eyes shift for a second to Jezzabelle Sweet. "I hear tell you got a stake in the Cromwell farm. Waterfront rights and a state park next door would go mighty good with them high-priced lots. Don't you expect they would?"

The deputy could feel the game warden's heat, the man's neck gone red as raw sirloin. The strip of land to the river would be the veteran's piece. How in the hell had that news come to the old captain to be hung out with the laundry flapping in this room, and yet he had missed the connection?

Jezzabelle Sweet. Right on the money, the deputy thought. And how *she* knew would be as tangled as the thickets closing in on her house in the swamp.

The deputy looked to his left, toward the end of the counter. The yellow coffee cup sat steaming. The screen door to the porch slammed and the veteran was gone. The deputy was surprised he hadn't at least heard the outboard spin to life. He pretended nonchalance and turned, walking away from the game warden. He eased himself out onto the porch. The deputy felt the chill of the damp wind blowing in from across the water. Low talking thrummed in the room behind him.

There in the distance, the veteran bent his back to the sweep of oars, rowing his skiff upriver. He looked back inside, down the counter. Loo leaned forward, her elbow parked beside a napkin dispenser, her hand cupping her chin, eyes on the game warden as he fished money from his pocket.

THE BROAD FILE SWEPT CLEANLY ACROSS THE CURVING bit of the ax head. Both blades now were scalpel sharp, so that when the veteran tested the edge, a line of blood appeared on the pad of his thumb. He smeared it on the ax's cheek.

The gentle bellied arc of the hickory handle, its helve, finished with a brief kickback in the opposite direction at the grip so that, in the style and design of a war club, the force of his swing would be multiplied. The patina of a thousand handgrips was settled into the oily grain of the wood. Its balance was perfect.

No droning, smoking chainsaw was a fit choice for his labor.

The veteran put down the file and held the ax up, turning it slowly. The morning sun glinted off the new edges he'd put on the bits, and he appreciated the shallow wedge angle going down to the beard, for it would cut deeper and cleaner. This was an edge tool for wood, but the veteran knew others like it had seen service as tools of war. Village blacksmiths of old had found them easy to make though sometimes took the time to fashion intricate designs into their broad sides.

He wondered how long this ax had been in the widow's family and what work it had seen, and he mulled over would he give it back to her once this day's work was done.

His mother had forbade him as a boy to walk into her house shouldering an ax, and on the one time, the first time, he had done so, she made him stop in his tracks and turn around three times then step carefully backwards and outside again. She had said it would bring bad luck to him and there was plenty of that to go around already.

In time, he had learned of more superstitions that followed axes from their ancient winged and socketed days, when stone axes were believed to be invested with the magic of thunder and used to guard buildings against lightning. Buried upright under the sill of a house, an ax kept away witches. A thrown ax could turn away a hailstorm. In a farmer's field, an ax with the cutting edge toward the skies saved the harvest from bad weather. An ax underneath the marriage bed promised male children.

This ax would make a gash that would be salved and hashed at supper tables for years, and there would be some bad luck to go with it. Of that the veteran was certain. On the other hand, this was a battle-ax and it would cleave away an enemy encroachment—whose ranks did not include trespassers onto the widow's land, himself among them.

These skulkers were part of the story of the tree, the pilgrims to Ghosthead Oak who crossed a barbed fence to get there were themselves wild by the nature of their act and therefore the kith and kin of the tree, its very idea. The veteran could not hold in his head, however, the image of a tourist licking an ice cream cone while reading the tree's description from a list of amenities on a three-fold brochure.

He stood from the smoothly sawn stump on which he'd sat and it was not lost on him, the irony of where he'd sat to hone the edge of his chopping ax. Nor did he forget what the widow said when she reminded him how many farmers sold off timber for the money to make another crop. For the clearing of new fields to plant. To settle a mortgage, or send a daughter to college. The disposition of any tree on her land was her right to decide.

And yet. This tree. This tree and no other tree.

He'd held a buddy, a man from Alabama, his leg blown off when their PBR had been ambushed by small arms fire and a satchel charge catapulted from the bank of the Song Ong Doc River. He had not even reached into his canvas pouch for wound dressing or morphine, only cradled him. As he screwed off the lid of his canteen to give him water, his friend's head on his knee, the dying man licked away blood, spat on the deck and said, "Right about here, this shit gets real specific, don't it?" Cloud-born philosophical quandaries do not fit when shrapnel tears into your belly.

The veteran shouldered the ax and set off to do his specific work.

He did not walk to Ghosthead Oak. He strode. Long strides. Purposeful. Had he dawdled, whistling, minding the zig-zagging dragonflies, and become distracted thinking how they are born swimming and live flying, he might have turned back. He had laid his hand to this plow, and the preachers told him no one who looks back is fit for the Kingdom of God. And no matter if he won the kingdom of the devil, his hand was bound to this deed.

His heels dug in, marking each step, and soon he was out of the woods and into the tall grass. Had he looked down then he would have seen deep footprints from his sprint three nights ago. But he kept his eyes ahead. The ax stayed on his right shoulder. His grip on the handle was cool.

Now he saw the tree.

Still his steps did not falter, nor did he hesitate to assume a wide stance within three feet of the trunk of the huge old tree. Only when he had wrapped both hands around the ax handle, only when he had extended the ax in front of himself and looked at the double-bitted head held at eye level did he still every muscle in his body. Because it flew into his mind to say a prayer.

What? In a breath, he considered and discarded, *In the name of the Father, the Son, and the Holy Spirit…*

Instead, he said, *Sonsofbitches!*

He swung the ax into the trunk of the tree with such a

ringing blow that the blade sank five inches, a downward cut. He wrenched the ax loose with a growl. When he matched the first cut upward from directly below it, a fist-sized chunk of oak flew from the tree and struck him in the chest.

A fire raced through him, igniting his muscles and bones and numbing his mind. Something hot and molten poured through him and the strength of ten men was behind each swing. Each slice from the ax severed water-conducting vessels in the cambium layer just beneath the bark. When his six-inch deep ring-around-the-tree was done, the tree would die of thirst. Ghosthead Oak could not be saved from this girdling technique used by woodsmen since axes were fashioned from stone.

The veteran's peripheral vision blurred and he could only see the sharp strike deep into the massive tree's furrowed bark. Sweat poured from him, and he ripped at his shirt. Back to work. His heart was a hollow knock behind his sternum. The curl of his grip on the hickory handle, his wrists and forearms, his arms and shoulders and his back, all a welded-together thing of coiled intent, like some mad scientist's machine got loose on the tree.

When the flesh-colored gash was a circle, completed, another circle plowed with his boot soles into the leaves and soil around the trunk, start to finish, the whole sorry business was done. And a man had killed the tree, Ghosthead Oak, in its fifth century, with a chopping ax.

The veteran switched his grip on the ax handle, lifting it

and letting it slide through his hand until the head was near his fingers. He curled his left hand into a fist and walked away from the tree. He did not look back.

THE WIDOW SAW HIM COMING ACROSS HER YARD, AND
her dog sensed his approach. She put up a mighty fuss,
barking and whimpering and scratching at the front door to
get outside and defend the place.

The widow dropped the gauzy curtain, wondering what
to do. She had taken the chainsaw he'd thrown across her
floor and had gone to the tree to return the saw and see
about the man, to find out if he really needed a doctor.

The hireling was gone when she got there.

She could see where the chainsaw had torn into the tree
and her heart heaved and she had thought she would be
sick all over again. She went home and built a fire that she
watched until the crackling blaze on the hearth died and
grew cold.

As she pulled back the curtain again and watched the
veteran hard-boot across the dirt drawing nearer to her
cottage, her own ax in his hand, her state of mind deter-
iorated as if some dark magic was worked on her. She could

not remember a time when she was so at the mercy of forces that threatened her sense of emotional and spiritual balance. She was afraid of the man climbing the steps onto her porch.

She tensed for a replay of the nasty kick he'd planted on the fragile door last night, seeing only now a splintered crack in the lower panel. The footsteps of the man on the porch went silent and she knew he stood opposite her door. When he knocked but gently, she almost fainted. Then his voice came easy and sincere through the wood of the door.

"Ma'am?"

The widow looked at her dog as it searched her face. She had no idea what she should do. So she answered the man.

"What do you want? I don't want to open the door."

"No need," he said. "I only need to say about a minute's worth, then I'm gone."

The widow clasped her hands together and drew them to her chest. She held her breath.

"I'm sorry for going off on you last night. I didn't mean to storm your home and scare you. Now I need to tell you that the deed is done. There might've been another way out of this. But it's done. We can't unmake what we did."

Her heart thunked so that she could not hear his words clearly, though such was unnecessary.

"It's done," he said again. She heard that.

"Finished." She heard that, too.

While the widow considered would she open the door, he left. When in a moment she did pull the door open to look out on the porch, the man was gone from sight. Her ax was leaned against the newel post at the bottom of the steps. What was *finished* poured a thickening air into her lungs that caused her to fall on the porch. The light was shut off from her eyes, and all the thoughts vanished from her head.

Someone standing a ways back from her, say under the live oak there with its shag of moss, might have thought the widow just died. But that would not have been right. Though it would have been right to say that her heart quit right then. Tiny doors and passageways in her heart were sealed. Rhythms were disturbed. Yearnings abandoned. But the widow went on living.

HE CROW HAD SEEN HIM DO IT, HAD WATCHED HIM DO IT before he did it. The crow had known the time was coming nearer when he fought the other one. When his shiny button fell on the ground.

She would not uncurl her toes from the thin branch even when the first blows of the ax sent electrical jolts into her feet, a metallic hum into her wings.

She had known the rowing on the river yesterday was bound with intent, would bring him to do what was written so long ago.

Her sharp yellow eyes had followed him as he emerged from the woods with a heavy black-bladed cutter, its curved edge the width of her wingspan.

She had held the button in her beak while he chopped. And chopped.

When each blow fell, she blinked her eyes.

When the last blow had fallen, she dropped the button, and it spiraled downward until it landed where he had lost it the first time.

And the heel of his boot had pushed the button into the soil.

It would not be found.

The relic was not lost.

THE LEAF THAT FELL, THE FIRST ONE TO DIE, WAS SMALL and green. In time, others would fall, all of the leaves would let go. But not in some leaf storm, though the big tree, when it had died, dry and brown, would look wind-stripped and hurricane battered. Ghosthead Oak's leaves would fall, tired, like thin jade scales from an aging dragon.

THE VIEW TILTED DOWN FROM A CRESCENT MOON TO the shiny Airstream trailer. Yellow light pooled on the ground around the open door, and a country music ballad, slow and sort of bluesy, maybe Lyle Lovett, filled the interior and drifted like smoke into the night air.

On the kitchenette table, a bottle of Tennessee sour mash.

Outside, wobbling down the sloping, wooded landscape, the veteran careened sideways, crashing into a thick pine. He fell sideways into the briars and the gathered leaves, and a broken stick gouged deeply into his cheek. He rolled onto his back and rubbed the pain in his face, blood mixing with the dirt in his palm.

Before he passed out, the stars seemed to him more luminescent than the night last fall, after the season's first northerly had swept the haze from the sky and he had shut down his outboard motor, put his head back on a boat cushion arranged in the bow of his skiff, let no anchor down—just drifting, drifting into the shallows and a whisper of marsh grasses reaching to the top of the sparkling night.

Tonight he drifted again, free-floating to the end of a slow-moving river of black.

But then he awakened underneath the curve of night sky and saw the widow sitting, leaned against a fat magnolia, her legs drawn up, eyes on him. The veteran might have spoken, but the whiskey fog rolled in on him again and there was no one there, only the soft earth cradling him warm under his back.

THE BIG CAT WAS INDISTINCT FROM THE SHADOWS OF the woods in darkness. It lay within several yards of the woman and her dog and the man on the ground. The gentle wind brought their scent to him and the panther lifted his nose and blinked his yellow gibbous eyes. It stood, but still. So still only its breathing signaled it a thing alive. And when it finally took slow steps, moving broadside to them on great paws with strength there to slap a crack in the skull of a dog, the woman turned her head and followed its going but did not otherwise stir or even budge. Nor did she rouse when its breath purled, a soft growl as from deep inside a cave.

THE VETERAN PUT HIS HEAD BACK AND GAZED AT THE wood ceiling in his Airstream and breathed into his nostrils the spicy-delicious smell of Cuban black beans. He had water going for some rice. Black and white, *Moros y Christianos*. The onions and garlic and cumin. He closed his eyes and drifted away again.

He was disturbed from his daydreaming by the snap of a twig from out toward the edge of the clearing. The veteran sat upright, peering out the open door into the noonday light. The deputy walked into view as the veteran stepped outside, crossing his arms.

"What the hell are you doing out here again?"

"Take it easy," the deputy said. "I remember. You are the man with the gun."

The veteran blinked, red-eyed and a little groggy.

"Miss Loo sent me. You forgot to pay your tab," the deputy said.

"You go to hell," the veteran said. "You got about ten

seconds to run back to the game warden."

"I won't be drawing any more of those paychecks. I'm on my way back to a reporter's desk. Stories are what I know. And there's a story here."

"Not one in my trailer. Last time. Get the hell out of here, or it may be an obituary that goes to press," the veteran said.

"Man, those black beans smell great," the deputy said.

"What?"

"This is where I worm my way closer to my subject over lunch," the deputy said, grinning. "Look, some barfly gave a tip on the tree and there are twenty big city dailies heading for that tree. No stopping that. I'm after something else." The deputy put his hands into his pockets. "I might never type a line of this. Or in twenty years I might write a book. Whichever. Who cares? The story's breathing now and so am I. Did you chop that groove into the trunk of the big oak?"

The veteran squinted in the deputy's direction.

"Maybe you are the whacked-out war nut I hear about. But crazy's an angle that works with what went down out there. What'd you use? A freaking Viking ax?"

"Who said I did it?"

"We're hearing a man walked into the newspaper office in Fairhope croaking that some crazy woman hired him to kill a giant oak tree and then sent somebody in on top of him to stop the work and assault him in the process."

The veteran cut his eyes at the deputy, but just as quickly returned his gaze upward, toward the blue sky through the tree branches. He continued to look there as he asked, "Your boss on the scene?"

"He's on his way. Got some kind of court order and plans to set up a base camp out there," the deputy said. "Said when the bastard returns to the scene of the crime, he'll have him to deal with."

"That's bullshit," the veteran said. "No charges will be filed."

"That's right. It's just some thrill for the game warden to deal with the media."

"It might not be as thrilling as he thinks," the veteran said. Then, "Damn, my beans." He trotted back toward the open door of the trailer. The deputy followed.

"Smells good," the deputy said, looking inside.

"You're lucky I didn't scorch my lunch yapping with you."

"I'm not kidding, I'd like a plate of black beans and rice. They smell like the beans I would always get at this joint in Miami, and haven't had any like it since."

"I give you some beans, you shut up and get off my place?"

"You mean I don't get a story?" the deputy asked.

"I mean you get a plate of beans. Then you get your college ass out of my trailer."

The deputy reached one more time: "You know there are foresters and tree experts from all over the world busting their heads trying to figure out how to save the tree? The game warden said something about an oxygen tent over the whole thing. It'll soon look like some post apocalypse scene just through those trees."

The veteran turned from the pot on the stove. He stood and massaged his temples and the top of his head, stirring his hair all around. He cocked an eye toward the table. The veteran motioned for the deputy to push back the chair and take a seat at the dinette table. He served two plates of black beans and white rice and two glasses of water. The veteran ate in silence. The deputy let his questions lie fallow. When the veteran's plate was clean of every last bean and every last grain of rice, he told the deputy to leave.

"Go on, get out."

"You made good beans," the deputy said, standing to go.

The veteran turned on his seat. "I don't like a game of twenty questions. I won't sit still for it any day. Don't think to come back out this way."

He rapped his knuckles on the table, jarring the flatware on the ceramic plates. "But here's this," the veteran said, "I put my nose where it didn't belong. I interrupted something that woman had free right to conduct. I put her in a fix. I just took it up where it was left off."

"And you want me to believe—"

The veteran struggled to quickly stand, and the deputy recoiled. The veteran balanced himself with his hands on either side of the empty plate on the table and leaned forward. His eyes telegraphed furious intensity.

"I don't give a damn what you believe," the veteran said, holding his voice low, which delivered even greater effect.

"But you're a fool to think you can pump a little ink through places where blood flows and get anything to live."

The deputy's face tilted down, and when he looked back up at the veteran, it was as if some odd transfusion had occurred, as though some elixir of privilege had been sucked out of the deputy and what was pumped back into him was equal parts surrender and humility.

"I'm sorry I bothered you," the deputy said.

"Just get the hell out of here," the veteran said.

T HE GAME WARDEN WAS IN CHARGE OF THE PERIMETER. This land—three acres inside a new chain link fence with Ghosthead Oak at the center—now belonged to the state. The proceedings for the state's right of eminent domain had been fast-tracked in a week according to a judge's order meant to make it legal and safe for the team of tree experts from around the world to set up shop. The game warden had told the county commissioners about the widow's .410 shotgun. He said she was an expert marksman. He told of trespassers' visits, how the tiny lead pellets had caused no fatal injuries but left scars and pockmarks.

The game warden escorted a Dodge van through the double gates, told the driver to mind the cords and hoses on the ground and park beside the other three vans sporting TV news logos.

"You guys are lucky," he said, as a crew of three men tumbled out. "You'll get shots of the big green house tent they'll put in place here in a minute right over the whole tree. Notice how all the little branches have been pruned off. It's down to the basics. What's going to happen under that tent will be the next crucial step in saving the tree. Like surgery in the ER."

The cameraman, the one with the bulky vest, asked about the huge polyethylene blanket spread over a section of newly mown ground, how such a feat as raising it into position might be accomplished.

"A helicopter," the game warden said. "That one coming from off yonder."

Everyone on the ground, the news people and tree experts and law enforcement officers around the tree, seemed hypnotized through the whole operation as the helicopter lowered a tether to men on the ground and the line was attached to the big piece of translucent plastic sheeting. Then the chopper lifted, taking the plastic up. Weights along its perimeter kept it from flapping. Long lines were also attached to the corners and sides so the men were able to spread the sheet as it was settled over the branches and draped to the ground.

"Now, you watch," the game warden said. Tent pegs were used to secure the whole affair. "They're staking it off so the wind won't get it, and then they'll pump in the right mix of oxygen and moisture and chemical potions to save this glorious oak tree."

A man asked, "Have you found who did the dirty work?"

"Not yet. But it won't take long. We knew where to start. The widow. She'll soon tell us who did this crime. No way she'll outsmart me."

The reporter produced a business card. "Call me first," he said.

The game warden took the card and stuffed it into his shirt pocket without even glancing at it. He pointed to a man in a white lab coat.

"That's the fellow right there who came up with the little stroke of a genius idea," the game warden said, pointing in the direction of the tree. "See along the gash where it looks like stitches? That's a bunch of green twigs stuck in holes drilled above and below the nasty vee chopped around the trunk. The sticks are held in there with wax. That way the tree can get water up to the leaves from down in the roots."

"Wow," the cameraman said. "I gotta get that. It looks like Frankenstein's neck, all sewn up."

"Yeah, that old bat thought she'd deny the good citizens of this state and our great nation the right to come and see this tree. Get their pictures made with it. But the stitches will save this tree, and she'll see who knows how to play the game."

The TV reporter was taking notes. "Game? I'm not sure," he said, "I understand what you mean—"

"Y'all better go catch the tree doctor before he locks himself up in that mobile lab of his. You'll have to listen careful," the game warden said. "He's from Norway, or someplace, and doesn't speak good English. But he can tell you the tree is going to live. That's the most important. Ghosthead Oak's got another five hundred years coming."

I N THE AFTERNOON SUN THE CROW'S BREAST SHONE SAPPHIRE
blue. She sat on an upper branch where the leaves were
going yellow at the edges. Some were brown. No one on the
ground—those moving between their trucks, disappearing
into and coming out of the oxygen tent—paid any mind to
the crow when she rose into the air and glided in a wide
circle to land on the ground.

She hopped among the leaves, turning one eye and then
the other to the brown acorns beneath its broad, round
breast. If anyone had been looking, they would have seen
the crow take one capped acorn in its beak and put its head
down and spread its wings as if in prayer.

No one looking on could have known the very acorn
the crow chose, that one alone, could have taken purchase
at this place. When the giant tree died, when it was pulled
down and hauled away, saplings from marked containers
would be transplanted into the soil that had known the
broad shade of Ghosthead Oak. But though the shoots set

out were the scions of the big tree and were nourished to supple strength and raised to a man's height, they would all perish. One after the other they would become brittle and skeletal and Ghosthead Oak Park would come to enclose three acres of ground where no oak tree would grow.

Anyone reflecting upon this might say such dark rich soil was rendered barren to show a wrong was done upon the place.

If anyone could have followed the flight of the crow that day, watched as she landed on a low rise within a clearing surrounded by marsh grasses and cattails, upon a certain spot of ground where no man had walked in three hundred years, they would have seen her drop the brown acorn and drive her beak into the damp earth there. They could have watched the crow take up the acorn again and drop it into the hole and immediately fly away.

But no one was watching.

THE DEPUTY DROVE TO THE WIDOW'S COTTAGE. He swung his legs out of the Scout and hopped to the ground. Before he got to the porch, he heard a car behind him. It was the widow. When he turned to face her, he saw the veteran in the passenger's seat. The deputy stood like a prisoner looking into an off-limits compound as both doors opened and the pair stepped out.

The widow stopped in front of him, crossed her arms as if hugging herself warm. But it was balmy and spring-like even though Christmas was in two days. The veteran did not look at the deputy and walked past. He looked over his shoulder as the veteran went and sat on a porch step. The widow's black dog joined him, sat at his feet facing him, his ears up. The veteran offered the back of his hand and the dog sniffed it, dropped her ears and lay down at his feet.

"I came to say goodbye," the deputy said. The widow nodded.

"Have you been to see the tree?" he asked.

She shook her head. "It's dying," she said.

"It is," the deputy echoed.

"They can't save it," she said.

"Maybe not," he said. The widow walked past him and sat on a step, too—one below the veteran. There was an arm's length between them.

"What will become of the land they took from you?" the deputy asked.

She said, "They will cart off the big tree a log at a time. Maybe sell them. When what's left is a stump, they'll grind it to make a place for a new tree." The widow fell quiet for a long moment.

"I expect the wood would make a beautiful table," the deputy said.

"That's so," she said and was quiet again.

The deputy's anchor failed then to hold and he lost himself in the waves of a day beyond an unknown horizon: He watches himself drag his chair close to a table and rub oil on a table in big lazy swirls, its honeyed boards so broad and thick they look carted off from a knight's mead hall. There are lines etched into the skin across his knuckles, lines that will get deeper with age. There are lines in the golden grain of the oak, light and dark striations of five hundred years' growth like some lost writing of ancient and mysterious tales of brave men and their impossible deeds.

He makes a circle with his right hand just to feel the cool wood.

In the twilight silence of an empty house, as shadows of evening rise up pictureless walls, he thinks about being dead, absent from this place, and wonders what of him will remain in the things he has touched. He rests his hands palms down in the middle of an oak plank twice as wide as any piece of oak a man can buy. Someone might ask him does he not want to maybe remove and re-saw the planks to make the table narrower. Someone might tell him it would take an army to haul the table.

And he'll say no, he isn't going to saw the boards.

Someone might ask him when he expects to seat twelve people for a meal.

He might say he'll call some people up.

Someone might tell him, You and that damn table.

He might say it's a bed. And laugh. But then get up and go to his bedroom and drag the blankets off, grab his pillow, and make it into a bed. Next morning, he might sleep in. He might lie there on the table and think about writing a book.

The widow spoke again and the deputy reclaimed his footing in her yard.

"My great-great-grandfather," she said, "he saw this day coming. He wrote about it, told that blood deeper than the underground rivers watering the big tree would cause it to be cut down." She paused, patted the dog's head, and then looked back at the deputy.

"I once thought he spoke of blood spilled in rage," she

said. "But it's the stirring of blood in the soul of us, in the soul of every one of us, shared by all the wild things in the woods." Still the deputy said nothing. Nor had the veteran looked in his direction.

"One time," she said, "you said you wanted to write a story about Ghosthead Oak. You will, I think." She paused, shook her head. "But it won't be the story you believe you see now."

The widow looked past the deputy across the scrap of ground beneath the moss-bewhiskered branches of the live oak in her yard, her lips thin, her eyes tired. He looked at them both, first one, then the other. He spoke quietly, with resignation.

"Probably half a hundred theories why a newspaperman types '30' at the end of his story," the deputy said. "But I can tell you this—" He looked at the widow. Her eyes dropped to the scattered brown leaves at the veteran's feet, as though she could guess where he was going with this. The veteran now fixed him with a metal stare through smoke from his cigarette.

The deputy decided he would not tell them anything.

The widow looked up at the veteran, who kept his gaze on the deputy until she put her hand on the toe of his boot, but lightly, tentatively. When the deputy took a step back to turn and leave, neither of them seemed to notice. His hands on the Scout steering wheel, the deputy gave a last look through his dusty windshield at the widow and the veteran. He had helped her to her feet, both her hands still in his. He drove away feeling like he once had driving past a church, hearing the choir inside singing, and the way the melody had faded to quiet not much farther down the road. The deputy shook his head and said aloud, "But they're still singing. And I don't care how many times I wrote '30' not once did a story ever end. Not once."

—The End—

IN A GRASSY COASTAL MARSH AT TWILIGHT, A PANTHER EASES from between a curtain of grass and a heavy undergrowth of fan-shaped palmetto palms, near a dead pine tangled with cypress vine, and walks a lazy circle around where the acorn lies in the hole, yet open. The big cat turns and approaches the tiny hole. Its giant black paw, pearl-white claws retracted, finds the hole and presses it closed. The panther vanishes into the grass. At the place where the crow walked with the acorn, on the spot where she dropped the acorn in a hole, there is a bulge in the soil. On a round spike of juncus grass, bending in a small wind, a single firefly blinks its light and the line that runs from here to there is joined and the circle is made round again. Light slips away to the west, and in its wake a million stars announce the coming night.

ACKNOWLEDGMENTS

My wife, Diana, and my kids—Emily, John Luke and Dylan—are my best story. I love the part where they all wonder why I don't have a real job. Best of all, that they stick with me even though I'm just a writer. Dylan's buddies, Drew and Raneil and Javon and Ethan all deserve a line in Mister Sonny's books. What did educator Marietta Johnson say? Prolonging youth is the hope of humankind. She's right.

Mac Walcott had plenty of advice on bees and goats and gentleman farming. Mac was the architect for our new public library, but has laid a much deeper and wider foundation of support and enthusiasm for the arts, and artists all over Fairhope.

Martin Lanaux and Skip Jones, as usual, were first-round readers of the early draft of this book and my writer pals Rick Bragg, Tom Franklin, Joe Formichella and Suzanne Hudson, Karen Zacharias, all of them put their pencil to these pages and made them better. Theodore Pitsios allowed me to get away to his beach house and share the muse playing in the winds off the Gulf of Mexico. David Adams Richards told me to write the story of the widow and the tree. William Gay is my great friend, and protector and defender of my confidence to trot out another book.

Barry Moser's wood engraving cover art validates the maxim, says all the words I wrote.

Mitchell Lee knows how to tinker under the hood of my computer.

MacAdam/Cage's David Poindexter and Patrick Walsh are the beating heart of publishing.

Thank you indie booksellers and friends: in Alabama, Karin and Keifer Wilson at Page and Palette, Jake Reiss at Alabama Booksmith, Thomas and Cheryl Upchurch at Capitol Books and News; in Louisiana, Britton Trice at Garden Districk Books, Tom Lowenburg at Octavia Books; and, in Mississippi, Diane Shepherd at Main Street Books, John Evans at Lemuria, Richard Howorth at Square Books, Jamie and Kelly Kornegay at Turnrow Books, the Reed family at Reed's Gum Tree Bookstore, and every member of their staffs. Thank you owners of hometown and neighborhood bookstores all over the country. Thank you internet biggies Amazon, Barnes & Noble, Borders, and Books-A-Million. Thank you book section editors and reviewers. Thank you book-thumping broadcasters. Thank you librarians. Thank you all for not letting these hard times become the great goodnight to book publishing everywhere.

My agent, Caroline Carter, is my champion and my hero.